WHERE THE
BLACK
FLOWERS
BLOOM

Clarion Books is an imprint of HarperCollins Publishers.

Library of Congress Cataloging-in-Publication Data

Names: Smith, Ronald L. (Ronald Lenard), 1959– author.
Title: Where the black flowers bloom / by Ronald L. Smith.
Description: First edition. | New York : Clarion Books, [2023] |
    Audience: Ages 8–12. | Audience: Grades 4–6. | Summary:
    When ghoulish creatures kill twelve-year-old Asha's
    guardian, her dying words launch Asha on a quest to stop
    an ancient evil, and along the way, she uncovers shocking
    secrets about the family she never knew and begins to find
    her place in the world as she discovers her own untapped
    powers.
Identifiers: LCCN 2022020970 | ISBN 9781328841629 (hardcover)
Subjects: CYAC: Magic—Fiction. | Good and evil—Fiction. |
    Orphans—Fiction.
Classification: LCC PZ7.1.S655 Wh 2023 | DDC [Fic]—dc23
LC record available at https://lccn.loc.gov/2022020970

Typography by Torborg Davern
22 23 24 25 26 LBC 5 4 3 2 1

First Edition

WHERE THE
BLACK
FLOWERS
BLOOM

RONALD L. SMITH

CLARION BOOKS
An Imprint of HarperCollins*Publishers*

PROLOGUE

A TOWER OF BLACK ROCK rose up on the desolate plains of the Burned Lands.

Its surface reflected sunlight, but no rays of warmth could penetrate its exterior. All life fled from this place but for one:

Shrikes.

A multitude of black birds, their hooked beaks as sharp as thorns, perched at the very top of the tower like sentries, their eyes taking in the dead landscape with a curiosity that could only be called human.

Deep inside, along twisting corridors, creeping black

vines snaked their way along the bare ground, as if to strangle anyone foolish enough to venture in.

This was the dwelling place of the Shrike, a sorcerer of great power. A tangled mask of dark feathers adorned his face, and his throne was carved from the bones of some unfortunate beast.

A Tokoloshe, a goblin of sorts, or some creature so corrupt and soulless it forgot its own name, stood before him.

"Speak," the Shrike said softly. "What have you learned of this . . . *child*?"

His voice was serene yet full of power. The creature groveled before the throne, his bulbous nose twitching. "Master, our spies say the child is with a troupe of players, an unruly group of tricksters and charlatans. She is a puny thing with hair as black as pitch."

The Shrike gazed upon his subject. "Look at me, worm," he said calmly.

With hesitation, the creature raised its eyes.

"Did I not say to send word of this child as soon as she was found?"

"Yes, my lord, but we only just learned of—"

"Silence!" the Shrike bellowed. "Find her. And bring her to me . . . *alive*."

The servant lowered his head even more, if that was possible.

"Yes, Master. I will not fail you."

"Begone!" the Shrike commanded him. "Leave my presence. I grow weary of your . . . groveling." He rested his head on a closed fist.

The Tokoloshe backed away, bowing the whole while, until the iron doors of the throne room clanged shut behind him.

Once free of the master's gaze, he raised a crude horn to his lips, and sounded a call to arms for the Shrike's terrible flock.

ONE

MARKED

ASHA COULDN'T STOP HER MIND from racing. It was her Telling Day, the time when a young person comes of age and leaves the playfulness of childhood behind. Suna had sent her into the forest to gather more bitter leaf—she was always sending Asha on an errand for something—and on the way, she'd passed by Kowelo, the masquerade troupe's juggler. He was a tall scarecrow of a man with a pointed black beard and a scar that ran from his earlobe to the corner of his chin. Asha always wondered how he came by it, but never got up the courage to ask. His skin was as black as ebony.

"Teach me to juggle," Asha demanded.

She must have asked this question a thousand times, but Kowelo always took it in good stride. He tossed the balls into the air, maneuvering three, then four. He balanced one on his nose as he answered. "Again?"

"Yes, again," Asha insisted. "I know I can do it."

The juggler laughed, sending the ball on his nose into his palm. "You must practice, child, if you ever really want to learn."

Asha scowled. "One, I'm not a child," she began, "and two, I *have* practiced."

This wasn't really true. Asha wanted to learn but she didn't have the one thing that would help her: patience.

"Okay, then," Kowelo said, letting the balls drop to his feet, "let's see what you've learned."

Asha picked up the balls and weighed them in her palms. *Now what did he say last time? Don't think of all three balls at once. Just think of them one at a time.*

She blew out a breath. *One, two, three.* She threw the first ball up into the air. Right as she was about to catch it, she tossed another, but much to her dismay, they both fell to the ground and rolled toward Kowelo's bare feet. He gave her a reprimanding grin. "You're going to make me look like a bad teacher."

Asha picked up the balls and tried again. This time she kept two balls in the air but couldn't get the hang of all three at once. "That's better," Kowelo encouraged her. "Keep practicing and one day you might take my job." He laughed then and, as if to mock her, picked up the three balls, added an empty bottle, and tossed them skyward, where they began a revolution of circles above his head.

"Show-off," Asha muttered under her breath. She picked up her basket and headed toward the forest that bordered the troupe's camp.

Asha often took long walks in the woods, when Suna wasn't ordering her around: *Asha, fetch more wood for kindling. Asha, gather some bean pods from the moringa tree, don't dawdle.* She was often annoyed by Suna's demands, but in truth, Asha loved the woman dearly. Twelve years past, Asha was told, Suna had found her in a brown wicker basket at the foot of her tent. Asha knew nothing of her parents and Suna always changed the subject when she brought them up. "You are an orphan, child," was all she said, her kohl-rimmed eyes intense but full of compassion. "A foundling."

But Asha knew there must have been more to the

story, and one day, she promised herself she'd find out.

Asha thought about her birth parents often and wondered why they'd left her with a traveling troupe. Was she not loved? Did they not want her? No matter, she consoled herself. Suna was the only mother she had ever known, and the assortment of griots, fortune-tellers, and illusionists was her family now.

Suna was Moorish, from a land in the far east of Alkebulan. Suna told her that at one time, her people ruled cities and kingdoms far and wide. They built palaces of gold and silver, with spires that reached to the heavens. They could even read the stars and navigate the seas. But Asha had never seen the sea, so she had a hard time imagining what that would be like.

Asha felt most at ease in the woods, away from chores and Suna's constant demands. It was always peaceful and green, and it gave her a sense of comfort she found nowhere else. Every now and then she would spy an antelope in the tall grass, or hear the distinct calls of long-tailed cuckoos and gray goaway birds.

Asha gathered all the bitter leaf she could find and rested against a moringa tree, its shade a pleasant respite from the blazing sun. She wondered what her Telling Day ritual would bring. She was twelve summers old, and tonight, on the eve of her thirteenth birthday, she would learn her true path in life. What would the great goddess, the Royal Lioness, reveal to her? Would she be marked with the crocodile, a sign of cleverness? Or perhaps it would be the spider's web, for creativity and knowledge. Suna possessed a wisdom knot on the back of her neck, a rare symbol of patience and intelligence. Asha thought about these things for a while until she found herself nodding off, her eyes beginning to close. With a start, she shook herself awake, picked up her basket, and returned to camp, anxious to learn her fate.

Asha pulled aside the brown flaps of her tent and walked in. Her eyes adjusted to the dimness. The tent was square, with wooden beams for support and heavy canvas for walls. It was a small dwelling, but seemed to contain everything one would need for a simple life: there was a table, two small chairs, bowls, plates, and spoons. A golden teapot with a brass spout sat on the table, complete with four filigreed cups. Colorful blankets and pillows took up every inch of the earthen floor where Asha and Suna slept. It was a little cramped at times, but still, it was Asha's home. At least for the time being. The troupe moved so often the tents were easily collapsible.

She set down the basket of bitter leaf on a red-and-green woven tapestry. The smell of fresh herbs and spices filled the air: coriander, sage, nutmeg, and cocoa. Suna looked up from a book she was reading. She wore a long robe of the deepest black, woven with beads of gold and silver. Most times a cowled hood shaded her face, but sometimes, like now, she went without it, revealing a cascade of raven-black hair that fell to her shoulders. Her skin was not as dark as Asha's but still brown, as if burnished by the heat of the sun. "I take it you got lost on the way?" she asked.

Asha stared at her feet. "No," she said weakly. "I mean—I had trouble finding leaves. I had to search for quite a while."

Suna raised a doubtful eyebrow.

Asha didn't like to lie, but she often stretched the truth, as she called it. "What is that?" she asked, pointing, trying to change the subject. "That book you're reading?"

Suna's dark eyes flashed for just a moment before she placed the book onto the table. She shot Asha a forced smile. "It is nothing, Asha. Now let's get you ready for the ceremony."

Asha sat at the small wooden table and waited while

Suna searched for her comb. Her eyes drifted to a basket in the corner that held small bottles plugged with cork stoppers. There were also neatly tied bundles of cloth that smelled rich and pungent—some smelled absolutely awful. Whenever Asha asked what they were, Suna only replied that they were tinctures and potions.

"Ah," Suna said, snapping Asha out of her thoughts. "Here it is."

She stood behind Asha and began to work on her hair.

"Ouch!" Asha cried, as a particularly stubborn knot was untangled. "That hurts!"

"Maybe if you combed now and then it wouldn't be so hard," Suna told her. "You have to look beautiful for your Telling Day, child. It is a very important occasion."

Asha sighed. She knew it was an important day and didn't need to be reminded. She was nervous enough as it was.

People were already gathered in a circle when Suna led Asha out of the tent. Asha looked out at the crowd and tried her best not to appear nervous, but inside, her heart was hammering in her chest. She wore a white smock that symbolized the purity of childhood, and her curly black hair, now free of tangles, sat on top of her head braided into three silky coils. Her feet were bare, a sign of humbleness. She had looked at herself in the small mirror glass before she left the tent. The person who stared back at her was unrecognizable. *Here goes,* she thought.

As was the custom on Telling Day, everyone wore a braid of green leaves from the marula tree around both wrists. This was to signify health and a long life for the newly marked. Music rose on the air—a wooden flute, a small drum, hand clapping, and the light tinkling of bells. It seemed to settle in Asha's soul, filling every part of her with joy as well as nervous anticipation.

The moon appeared in the darkening sky. A trickle of sweat ran down Asha's back. She looked around at the assembled mass and picked out Obo, the troupe's bullwhip master and overall guardian. If any trouble was met on the road, Obo was the one to put an end to it, and quickly. He carried a gnarled pine staff, but his specialty was the whip. He performed all kinds of tricks and feats with it—shattering bottles with one strong lash, pulling down high branches to get at ripe fruit, and cracking it in the air so loudly it could bring a crowd to silence. Asha's earliest memories were of the big man lifting her over his head with one arm as she screamed and dangled in the air above him. He wore rings in both ears and on his fingers, and even had one through his nose. A choker of bronze always circled his neck. Asha asked him about it once, and he'd told her that he'd been enslaved long ago and wore it as a reminder of his freedom. She didn't really understand, though. If he was free, then why did he still wear it?

Suna raised her right hand.

The music fell quiet and all murmuring ceased. Asha imagined that many here remembered their own Telling Day and the nervousness that came with it. She swallowed hard.

Suna took her hand and led her toward the throng. Asha felt as if each footstep was a mile. Suna halted and the group formed a circle around them. Asha thought of a sheep being herded into a pen. She looked at the faces staring back at her. She'd known them all as long as she could remember. They were one big family. But right now, Asha felt alone, as if no one could possibly understand what she was going through, even though she knew that wasn't true.

"Friends," Suna began, her arms held out in welcome. "We are gathered here in the presence of the gods for our friend and sister, Asha. She shall be marked this day and her path in life revealed.

"Safara," Suna called.

Asha scanned the crowd until she found Safara. She was a year younger than Asha, with dusty brown skin and unusually long eyelashes. Her Telling Day would soon be upon her as well. Asha tried to smile but she couldn't will her face to move.

Safara stepped forward quietly, carrying a stone bowl with both hands. She paused in front of Suna, who dipped her fingers into the cool ceremonial water. Asha closed her eyes and Suna turned to face her.

"By the Royal Lioness," Suna began, and dabbed Asha's forehead. "By the Great Leopard Watcher," she continued, touching Asha on one cheek. "By the Zebra," she said, touching the other cheek, her voice calm and hypnotic. "By the Ibis"—she lifted Asha's chin gently—"and by the wings of the Sea Eagle, today, you ascend to womanhood."

There was a pause. Asha heard wind sighing through the trees. Suna handed the bowl back to Safara and then made an intricate sign with the fingers of her left hand. "By the Five," she said solemnly.

"By the Five," echoed the crowd.

"Open your eyes, child," Suna said.

Asha did as Suna asked. The moon was now a silver orb in the sky, casting light upon the onlookers. She turned both palms up, wondering if her mark would appear there. She lifted the billowy sleeve of her smock and searched her forearm. Nothing.

She did the same with the other arm. Nope. She glanced at Suna, startled. Would her mark not appear? Did the gods not love orphans?

Suna walked toward Asha and took her hands in hers. She turned them over, studying her palms and forearms. She seemed nervous, Asha noticed, without her usual air of calm confidence. She ran her finger along the smooth brown skin at the nape of Asha's neck. The crowd was beginning to grow uneasy. Doubtful murmurs rippled on the air. Asha looked at Obo but his face was blank.

"Where is it?" Asha asked, her voice trembling. "Suna, where is my mark? Is it a crocodile?"

"Shh," she whispered. "It will be all right, child. Come with me." She took Asha by the hand and led her away to the sound of murmuring voices.

Inside the tent, Suna poured Asha a warm drink, which she took with both hands and gulped down quickly.

"Let us get a closer look," Suna said. "Take off your smock, Asha."

Asha pulled the smock over her head and Suna walked around to her back. Asha took a deep breath. Her nerves were rattled.

"By the Five," Suna whispered.

"What?" Asha cried. "What is it? Is it my mark?"

"Yes, child, you have been marked . . . by the Five, you have been marked."

"What is it?" Asha demanded again, craning her neck around. "Tell me!"

Suna traced her slender fingers along the great tree that spread out from the center of Asha's back. A baobab tree, with tangled roots that blended seamlessly into Asha's brown skin. Her spine was the trunk, rising up to gnarled branches that bloomed into clouds of green leaves on her narrow shoulders.

"It is a tree," Suna said quietly. "Your mark is a tree, Asha. A baobab." She paused and her voice grew solemn. "What strange omen have the gods revealed?"

TWO

OMENS

ANSWERS COULDN'T COME soon enough.

It had been nearly a week since Asha's Telling Day, and the only thing she learned from Suna was that the baobab tree was known as the Tree of Life, and grew in the Dry Lands far to the east.

In her tent, Asha was bending herself into an odd shape in front of the small mirror glass to get a closer look at her mark. She could only see part of it—a creeping green vine that ran up her right shoulder blade.

Suna told her not to worry, and that she would have to do a little more studying to understand what Asha's mark truly meant. So Asha went about her days as if nothing was unusual, although some members of the troupe, those she did not know well, eyed her warily whenever she crossed their paths. They didn't know what her mark was—it was considered impolite to ask if it wasn't visible—and they were all curious. Asha saw it in the way they stared at her with long, questioning looks.

She was grateful that Obo was unconcerned, even though he didn't know what her mark was, either. "It just means you're special," he said one day, sharpening a curved, short dagger on a whetstone. Asha didn't know if she believed that or not. She was beginning to see her strange mark as a curse or hex of some sort. Everyone born on the continent of Alkebulan knew what their mark meant. It was what determined your path in life. Obo's mark was easily understood. It was a war horn, a sign of strength and readiness, two traits he had shown on many occasions.

"But I don't understand," Asha complained. "Suna still hasn't told me anything. She's supposed to know all about this stuff, isn't she?"

Obo turned the dagger over and continued to sharpen it, the blade making a grating sound as he drew it across the stone. "Suna is very wise," he said, without looking at her. "She will find out what it means. Don't trouble yourself, Asha. Now run and fetch my oilcloth, eh?"

Asha sulked. Another errand. *Will they never end?*

Suna threw the oval stones into the clay basin again. The clear water made rippling circles as the stones slowly sunk to the bottom. They made the shape of the five gods: a circle with one point in the middle. *Strange*, she thought. The last few casts had shown the same sign.

She was shocked when she first saw Asha's mark, for she had traveled far and wide, from the old country of the Moors to the continent of Mercia, and had never seen anything of the sort. What could it mean? She sighed and gathered up the stones, then went to find ink and parchment.

Sister Rima,

The child who I sheltered twelve years past has had her Telling Day. Strange, but her mark is a symbol I have never seen.

I have searched the old signs but to no avail. Her mark is a tree, a great baobab, which graces her back. I thought that perhaps you, or one of our sisters abroad, has some knowledge of this. Please send word.

May the Royal Lioness protect you,

Suna

Suna made the sign of the five gods, passed her hand over the parchment, and watched the writing slowly fade, only to be seen again by those who knew how to reveal it.

Outside, the night was quiet, but for the soft clicking melody of a *kora*, a type of small, wooden harp. Kowelo and a few others huddled around a crackling fire, where roasting meat sent wisps of smoke up into the air. If they had been paying attention to their mistress, they would have seen her walk to the edge of the wood, murmur a few strange words, and then utter a sharp command. A moment later they would have heard a rustling in the trees and seen a great harrier hawk swoop down from the boughs, yellow eyes gleaming. But Suna's footfalls were soft and not a soul at the fire stirred.

The hawk settled at her feet and Suna knelt and placed the rolled-up parchment in the band around one of its legs. *"Kuruka,"* she said.

The hawk set off, its wings taking to the night air with great thrusts, until it vanished in the distance. Suna stood and watched until it faded in the northern sky.

Asha turned the teacup over and placed it on the saucer. She rotated it clockwise three times, stopping at every rotation when the handle faced her. Finally, she tapped the bottom of the cup with her index finger and let it rest for a moment on the surface. To the untrained eye, it was a tea reading, but Asha knew it by another name, one that Suna had explained to her. It was called scrying, the art of divination, also known as tasseography, a skill Suna had learned in her own land, and now Asha was her apprentice.

She peered into the cup. Candlelight revealed clumps of black, wet tea stuck to the bottom and sides. She furrowed her brow. The stranger before her twitched and scratched his narrow nose. This was her first time reading the leaves alone. She usually sat at Suna's side and watched as her mistress wove a tale of prophecy for the men and women who came to have their fortunes revealed.

"Well?" the man asked, his voice raspy.

Asha bit her lip. "It's not good," she finally answered.

"What does it mean, girl?" the man pressed her, irritated now. His mark was a fern—a sign of endurance and hardship—and it ran from behind his ear to a tangle of hair at the base of his neck.

"You must leave your home," Asha said. "If you stay here, you are in danger. Look." She pointed to one fleck of tea that looked like any other. The man leaned in, curious. "This is a dark omen," Asha continued. "You must flee. And soon." She settled back in her chair.

The man took a greedy swig from a bottle of murky brown liquid. The odor was unbearable, and Asha wrinkled her nose. It smelled like acrid smoke from a green fire. He wiped his mouth with the back of his hand. Asha looked to the cup again, and noticed a pattern on the side, about halfway down. "This area is the present," she told him. "The top of the cup is the future, and the bottom is the past." She pointed. "This is a ladder, which means travel." She turned the cup to the other side. "And here. This is the kettle, which means . . . death."

"Hmpf," the man grumbled, standing up. He fished in his pocket and two copper coins clattered onto the table. Now he leaned in close—so close Asha could smell sap-brew on his breath. "If I find you have lied, girl, I'll have your head."

Asha saw the glint of a dagger in the folds of the man's shabby clothes. "The leaves speak truth," she said, eyes straight ahead, showing not the slightest trace of fear. The man snorted, swept aside the tent flaps, and stumbled out, leaving the cloying smell of sweat in his wake.

Asha closed her eyes and let out a breath, glad to be rid of him. She wasn't scared. Suna wouldn't send anyone who was *truly* dangerous her way. She was also close by, but unseen in her neighbor's tent.

Asha set the cup aside and noticed the wet clumps on the saucer. They made a curious shape. *A bird?* The wings were clearly visible, even the feathers. And there—could those be small black eyes, looking out at her?

Asha blinked. The wet tea remnants seemed to be . . . *moving.* Surely she was seeing things, but when she looked again, her heart raced. What could have been a beak opened and then closed. The candle sputtered and hissed as if blown by an unseen breath. She continued to stare, like an invisible force was bending her to its will. Her eyelids drooped and her head began to sway. The room grew cold. Blood pulsed at her temples. The flap of the tent rustled and Suna stepped through just as Asha's head fell upon the table.

"Asha!" Suna cried, rushing to her side and lifting her head. "What has happened, child?"

Asha took a moment to speak, trying to gather her wits. "I don't know," she finally said, her head as heavy as a stone. "The leaves . . . it was a bird. It . . . it looked at me!"

Suna glanced at the mound of wet tea, then picked up a pinch and rubbed it between her fingers.

"I felt like I was falling," Asha said. "I couldn't look away!"

Suna continued to stare at her smudged fingers. "It's all right, child," she said, and caressed Asha's brow. "It's going to be all right."

But somehow, Asha knew her words were far from the truth.

THREE

THE DARKNESS

T HE TROUPE MOVED ON as always, from small villages to larger towns. Suna was the one who seemed to know just what a town or village needed to prosper, and she was paid handsomely for it. Most times they wore masks and put on simple performances, or prayed and danced for good weather or protection from evil. Asha watched most of these celebrations from afar but didn't join in. She just couldn't get up the nerve to sing or dance with wild abandon the way she had seen the others in the troupe do many times before.

They soon came to a town indistinguishable from

any of the others they had visited over the years. They set up their tents and wares in a clearing on the edge of a dense wood thick with quiver trees.

Asha sat with her back against the broad trunk of a tree and stared up at a sky the color of lead. For weeks she had felt out of sorts, as if she were on the edge of some great cliff, and if she weren't careful, she would fall and never have a chance of recovering.

There was still no news of what her mark meant. Suna had become even more secretive and elusive, and Asha's many questions were dismissed with a wave of her hand. She knew something, though, Asha could tell. More than once, when she came upon Suna by surprise at the small table, she had shuffled her papers and pushed her books away, as if she were hiding something. *Is it about me?* Asha wondered.

She hadn't touched the tea leaves since her fainting episode, but she thought about it constantly, even in dreams. She saw the bird perched in trees, its black eyes gleaming, the sharp beak opening and closing.

Asha kept the dreams to herself. She thought she had given Suna enough to worry about. But she knew that it meant something. And one day, she would find out— maybe when she finally understood her mark.

▲ ▼ ▲

Asha lay asleep, her chest rising and falling slowly.

Suna lit another candle, then pulled her cloak around her. The air was cool, which was unusual for this time of year, when nights were usually as sweltering as the day. She glanced at Asha again and then reached for the roll of parchment, a reply from Rima:

Dear Sister,

After much divination, I have found that the baobab tree is one of the sacred symbols of our old friends, the Aziza, whose tribes are now lost in the forgotten years of history. I do not know why your foundling carries this mark, but surely it must mean something of great importance. I will write again, if I discover more.

May the Royal Lioness protect you,

Rima

"Aziza," Suna whispered, setting down the letter.

A clamor of voices arose outside the tent. Asha bolted up from sleep. "What's going on?" she asked sleepily.

"Wait here, child," Suna whispered.

Suna put the parchment away and hurried out to discover Obo, Kowelo, and a few other men and women from the camp, with grim faces and weapons at the ready.

"What is it?" she asked, taking in their grave looks. "What is happening?"

"Kowelo saw something in the night sky," Obo replied. "Something . . . *unnatural.*"

"*Unnatural?*" Suna ventured.

"Like a cloud," Kowelo said. "A black cloud, racing across the moon."

Suna looked at Kowelo. The juggler's eyes were wide with fear.

"What is it?" a small voice asked.

Suna turned around. Asha had crept up behind her silently, curious about the commotion.

"Asha, what are you doing here, child? Go back inside!"

"What is it?" she asked again, gazing into the distance.

Against the dark sky, a black shape was indeed moving—faster than an ordinary cloud. Suna sniffed the air. Asha heard a high-pitched hum that seemed to swirl around her head, a buzzing, frantic whirlwind. "It's getting closer," she said.

"Take shelter!" Suna suddenly cried, reaching out for Asha. But as they fled for safety, the oncoming cloud burst, and out of it flew a swarm of black birds, their wings beating the air in thunderous unison. *Caw!* they cried. *Caw! Caw!*

Asha threw her hands up in front of her face. Suna did the same, but before the birds attacked, they swirled into smoke, and from that smoke came the shadowy forms of men, dressed in robes of black.

Asha didn't understand what she was seeing. *Birds, turned into men?*

"The Shrike!" Obo cried.

Suna pulled Asha to the edge of the wood. Asha saw a look in her eyes she had never seen before. It was fear. "Stay here, Asha! This is too dangerous. Do not move!" And then she darted away, back to join the others.

Asha breathed in big gulps of air. She had heard of strange things in the world, evil beings that lurked in dark places, but *here*? In their camp?

She closed her eyes and made a silent prayer to the Five. If only she had something to fight with: poison darts, a blade, anything. But she had no weapon of any sort, except for her small fists, and they were no use at all. She peered out into the night.

Kowelo, Obo, and the others rushed forward. The shadow men swirled and moved in ribbons of black. Some carried silver swords, while others wielded spears. But their faces were what was most strange, if anything could be stranger than birds turned into men. Instead of noses they possessed sharp beaks, which opened and closed with shrieking cries.

Asha shuddered, remembering her fainting episode and the bird face that had haunted her dreams.

She watched as Obo lashed out with his whip, circling one of the creature's necks. The strange beast clutched at its throat, clawing for breath. Obo pulled it forward until it fell at his feet, scrabbling in the dirt. Asha had to squeeze her eyes shut when Obo reached for his blade because she knew what was coming next.

Chaos spread quickly. She saw Kowelo try to block one of the creature's sword thrusts, only to be surprised by another who attacked from behind.

"No!" Asha cried, as Kowelo fell to the ground, a sword in his back.

I have to do something! she thought. *I can't just stand here and watch my family die!*

Obo lashed out with his whip again, cutting the ghostly black figure who had stabbed Kowelo to shreds, as if it was made of smoke. *What are they?*

Suna, Asha thought with dread. *Where is she?*

The night sky was suddenly lit by bright, shining symbols. Gold and yellow sparks danced in the air. Asha raised her hand to her face, shielding herself from the blinding light, and when she opened them, she saw Suna, her arms raised to the heavens, crying out in a language Asha didn't understand. The hair on the back of her neck prickled.

A great gust of wind rose and the creatures flew backward, as if the claws of the Royal Lioness had struck them. Asha stared, shocked. *Suna knows magic?*

Before she had time to comprehend the enormity of what she had just seen, a human-shaped shadow, deeper than the deepest black, appeared on the outer edge of the forest. And it was coming toward Suna.

"No!" cried Obo, rushing to her side.

But it was too late.

Suna grasped her neck and fell to the ground.

Asha rushed through the trees, thorny branches scratching her face, but she didn't feel them.

"Asha, no!" Obo cried. "Stay back!"

But Asha did no such thing.

Instead, she thrust out her arm as she ran, her open palm facing the strange shadow.

"Back to the darkness!" she cried.

The shadow creature . . . burst.

A cloud of black ash rained down where it had stood just moments before.

Asha ran to Suna's side.

"No!" she cried, taking Suna's head in her hands, the shaft of a poison dart stuck in her neck. "Suna! Wake up! It's gone! I killed it!"

Obo ground his teeth and spat blood. He looked at Asha as if he had never seen her before. "By the Five," he whispered, and then seemed to come back to himself, and knelt down to help.

"You did well, my child," rasped Suna. "Hazelfire . . . so strong." Asha thought for a moment that Suna wanted to laugh but didn't have the strength. "I should have known," she went on. Her eyes were growing dim, but Asha saw a smile behind them. "Do not fear," Suna whispered. "Come . . . listen."

Asha lowered her head and, through a haze of tears, looked upon Suna's face. She was so close she saw green and brown flecks swirling in her eyes, something she had never noticed before.

"Now I know it," Suna said, her breath shaky.

"What?" Asha sobbed. "Know *what*?"

"Your mark," Suna whispered. "The tree. Seek the Underground Kingdom. Where the black flowers bloom."

And then, she closed her eyes.

FOUR

INTO THE WILD

NOOO!" ASHA CRIED, as Obo pulled her away from Suna's lifeless body. Warm, salty tears streamed down her face. "You can't die!" Great sobs welled up in her throat.

Asha stood in the ruin of their camp. Shattered. Her knees were weak. The ground was strewn with the bodies of her friends and companions. She looked to the edge of the wood, waiting, perhaps, for survivors to appear. But no one did. It seemed that only she and Obo remained; the rest were either dead or had fled quickly, in fear of the creatures that had attacked them.

"Come, Asha," Obo consoled her, laying a firm hand on her shoulder. "We must lay her to rest. I am sorry, child."

She couldn't move. Her stomach twisted into a knot. It was a pain she had never known before, a gnawing, terrible emptiness. Suna was dead, as was Kowelo. She didn't understand. How could this have happened? What were those creatures? Where did they come from? Her head swam with a thousand questions, but she could get no answers.

Obo built up a fire, while Asha sat on a tree stump, broken.

"We must do this quickly, Asha. Those . . . things may be back."

"*Why?*" Asha finally spoke, almost as if in a trance. "Why did this happen? What were they?"

Obo walked away from the growing fire and knelt by her side. He took her hand. "I don't know, Asha, but you have to be strong. That's what Suna would have wanted."

She put her arms around his massive frame.

"You can do it, Asha. Be strong. You destroyed it. Remember? That shadow thing." He paused and lowered his voice. "How did you . . . how did you do that, child?"

Asha suddenly remembered, as if in a dream, the words that had escaped from her lips. *Back to the darkness.*

She felt tired, drained of energy. She opened her mouth to speak but her head slumped to her chest.

Darkness.

Everywhere.

She was cold. Colder than she had ever been. A chill that seemed to grasp her heart in an icy fist.

She saw a flock of black birds take flight from the peak of a dark fortress, a bloodred moon glowing behind it.

She saw a giant creature with the head of a hyena crashing through the forest, the ground beneath its feet thundering . . .

And finally, she saw a mask, with bristling feathers around the eyes.

Asha, a voice whispered; a strange, calm voice, one she had never heard before.

Asha . . .

"Asha!" Obo cried, shaking her. "Wake up, girl!"

Asha opened her eyes. Obo's face loomed in her vision. He held the back of her head as her breathing calmed.

"What happened?" she asked.

Obo heaved a heavy sigh. "One minute you were talking and the next you passed out. Your head just kind of . . . fell."

"Here," Asha said. "Let me get up."

Obo helped her, but she still felt as if she could collapse. Her head was throbbing. "Drink this." He handed her a flask and Asha raised it to her lips and took a long swallow. It was water, cool and sweet, and it seemed to help her regain her senses. "The words," she whispered. "Back to the darkness. I don't know where they came from."

"They came from you," Obo said grimly.

Asha shuddered. The words had come into her head unbidden. Something inside her had unleashed a raging river and she couldn't stop it. *That shadow creature was killed by my words. How could that be? Was it magic? Suna used magic, too. The symbols appeared above her head and then there was a great wind.*

"The Shrike," Asha whispered. "That's what you said. What's a shrike? What does that mean?"

Obo let out a tremulous breath. "Did you see them? They were birds, Asha. Birds turned into men! Only a sorcerer can do that!"

Asha was confused. She had heard of sorcerers and demons, but she thought they were all just stories, tales that Suna and the griots told to paying customers. Judging by the fear in Obo's eyes, he thought differently. "The Shrike," she said again. "What is it?"

Obo toed a piece of splintered wood at his feet. He let

36

out another breath. "They say he is a demon who feeds on the blood of others. Some say he has a tower far away in the Burned Lands. Those birds were under his power, girl. Shrikes. They call them butcher birds because they impale their prey on sharp branches and then . . . *feed*." He shook his head. "They turned into men. By the Five!"

Dread settled over Asha, like a dark web of fear. How could birds turn into men? She swallowed hard and recalled again her fainting spell after the scrying. She had seen birds, and a tower . . . and there was a voice that had called out to her.

Asha.

"Come, Asha," Obo said. "We must lay them to rest."

Asha made the sign of the five gods over the bodies of her dead family and friends, who were shrouded in cloth gathered from one of the ruined tents.

"Royal Lioness," she began quietly, with more strength than she thought she had, "Goddess of Life and Death, please take our companions into your great dominion. Watch over them and keep them safe on their journey." She stepped back from the pyre. "By the Five," she said.

"By the Five," echoed Obo. He lit the pyre with a torch.

Asha watched the flames engulf the mound of the dead. Black smoke rose into the air to become lost in a star-speckled sky. Obo held back tears, his jaw clenched, his eyes cloudy. Only then did Asha realize how much he had been struggling, trying to be strong for her. She wept quietly.

Obo wiped his face with an ash-smudged hand. "It is done. We must leave, Asha. Now."

Asha met his eyes. "Wait a minute," she said quietly, and walked toward her tent. One of the cloth coverings in the front was slashed and torn, but everything inside remained untouched.

Asha stood for a moment, her eyes passing over everything that had made this place her home. It felt as if she were looking at things through a gray fog. She came back to herself. There was no more time. They could come back, Obo had warned her.

She stepped in, picked up a woven bag, and absently began to stuff a few things into it: a handful of nuts, a wooden giraffe Suna had carved for her, a pillow, and another shirt.

Asha looked at Suna's side of the tent from the corner of her vision. Hesitantly, she walked the few steps to stand beside the small table. She picked up the comb that Suna used on her Telling Day. Her eyes stung but she fought back the tears.

A few other items were scattered on the table. A feathered quill and ink jar, a small bowl of stones, various colored beads, green sprigs from an unknown tree, and a book. The same book Asha had seen Suna writing in on several occasions.

I shouldn't, she told herself.

She bit her lip, thinking. Suna raised her to be honest, not a thief.

But I only want to look at it, she reasoned. *There might be something in there that can help us.*

She picked up the book.

It was made of rough parchment. A sturdy piece of wood served as the spine, lashed with small threads of rope. There were no words or images on the cover. She lifted a finger to turn the page . . .

"Asha," Obo called.

Asha spun around.

Obo stood just outside the entrance.

"We must go now, child. Hurry."

Asha stuffed the book into her bag.

FIVE

SECRETS REVEALED

T HEY FLED THE CAMP that night, taking whatever supplies they could salvage from the various tents: food, clothing, blankets.

"What are we going to do?" Asha asked. "Where will we go?"

"I'm not sure," Obo answered, his face set into a hard grimace. "But first we must travel as far from here as we can."

They had no choice, Asha realized. They had to flee. What she really wanted to do was sit and cry, but she couldn't. That wouldn't help them at all.

The trail ahead of them was dark, and the moon was dim, casting a faint light between the trees. Asha's footfalls were loud in her ears. Every now and then she imagined she heard howling, but Obo assured her it was only the wind. That didn't relieve her growing fear. She imagined a great, hungry wolf with teeth as sharp as daggers lurking in the woods.

She couldn't get the image of the mysterious attackers out of her mind. "Obo," she asked quietly. "Did you know that Suna was a magician? She sent wind from the sky."

"The ways of Suna were always a mystery, Asha. I don't understand what she did, nor the words you spoke." He paused. "These are strange times."

Asha wanted to ask more, but she knew Obo was just as confused and troubled as she was.

After two hours of traveling, she felt like she could fall asleep on her feet. Even though the troupe had always made their homes near villages, Obo thought the one nearest their now-ruined camp was still too close to danger. "We'll head farther north," he said. "I know of another small town. They're a nice enough folk; hard-working and friendly to strangers. We will rest there tomorrow."

Asha felt relief at the prospect of stopping. She was

exhausted, moving through the world like a weary ghost. Finally, when she could go no farther, they came to a stop and spread their bedrolls onto the hard ground. Obo didn't want to start a fire for fear of being noticed, so they made do with an end of dry bread each, along with jackfruit and papaya. Obo reclined against a tree, his knotty pine staff resting across his legs. Asha wrapped herself in blankets and shivered against the cold, all the while thinking of Suna as she lay dying.

Moonlight shone down through the trees. Asha stirred and sat up. She glanced at Obo a few feet across from her. His massive chest rose and fell, his breath coming in soft snores.

Quietly, Asha reached for the woven bag at her side. She looked at Obo once more and pulled out the book.

A night bird whistled, giving Asha a start. "Forgive me, dear Suna," she whispered. "I just need to know what's in here."

She stared at the blank cover for a moment, and then she opened it.

A shock ran through her body.

There, in Suna's spidery script, was Asha's name,

printed in the center of a page. Small sketches surrounded it. Asha's fingers brushed the rough paper. One
of the drawings showed a small person with dark hair
and black eyes. The word *Aziza* was scribbled next to it.

"Aziza?" Asha whispered.

She flipped to another page. Here was a sketch of several tunnels, winding their way to points unseen. Next to
it she saw the words *Underground Kingdom.* She let out a
long, stifled breath. She had no idea what all this meant,
but she remembered Suna's final words. *Seek the Underground Kingdom. Where the black flowers bloom.*

"She whispered it to me before she died," Asha said,
still staring at the page. "What does it mean?"

"What?" Obo asked, rousing from his slumber.

Asha gulped. She hadn't even realized she had spoken aloud.

"Asha," Obo said, sitting up. "What is that? What are
you reading?"

Asha closed her eyes and opened them again. She
couldn't hide this from Obo. They were friends, and,
more importantly, he might know what some of Suna's
writing meant.

"A book," she said flatly.

"What kind of book?" Obo asked, standing up. He

seemed to tower above the trees, a giant in the forest.

"From Suna. I got it from our tent."

Obo walked the few short steps toward her. Moonlight spilled down on them, just enough to see by.

"Where is the Underground Kingdom?" Asha asked.

Obo wrinkled his brow. "Underground Kingdom? I don't know, Asha. Here, let me see it."

Asha handed him the book and he thumbed through it, his huge fingers nimbly turning the pages. "Underground Kingdom," he murmured. "This looks like tunnels of some kind."

"But where?" Asha asked.

Obo's eyes roamed over the pages. "Aziza," he whispered. "I know this word. I've heard stories of these folk from childhood tales."

Asha sat up further. "You have? Who are they?"

"*Were*," Obo replied. "Some say they were here before the world began. They lived in the deep forests and knew the language of the wind. Small they were, like children, with dark eyes and fierce weapons, to protect them from the coming of humans."

Asha had never heard of such tales. *Why did Suna write about them?* "What happened to them?"

"Long dead now," Obo said, handing the book back

to Asha. "If they ever existed at all."

Silence descended. Asha searched for what to say. "My name's in that book," she finally said. "Why?"

Obo lumbered back to his blanket and bedroll. "Suna was a mysterious woman, Asha. I do not know. She had many secrets."

Secrets, Asha thought. *I will find the answers. I must!*

SIX

SPRIX

ASHA AWOKE WITH A PAIN in her back. She stretched and yawned and rubbed her eyes. The sky was a cloudless blue, and for a moment, she made to smile, then suddenly remembered where she was and why. They had been attacked. Suna and Kowelo were dead, killed by the Five knew what.

She joined Obo a short distance away. It was still unsafe to light a fire, so they shared papaya and bread. Asha chewed her food as slowly as she could because she didn't know how long it would have to last. She brushed the twigs from her hair. It was a mess. She would have to get Suna to comb out the—

Her eyes suddenly watered.

I'd do anything to hear her voice again, Asha thought. *Even if I were being scolded.*

This time, she did cry.

They packed up their bedrolls in silence and set off. Asha looked around with wide eyes. Her travels had never taken her so deeply into the forest before. She peered up at the sky every few moments, expecting to see another storm of birds diving to the earth. Shrikes, Obo had called them. Birds turned into men with shadowy robes. She shivered.

The woods soon began to thin and the trail was replaced by a worn path of crumbled gray stone that marked the entrance to a village. Asha was relieved. Her feet were aching and her small pack was like a weight of stones on her back. She was dirty, too, but she didn't care much about that, though she did want to wash her face and put on a clean shirt.

"Here we are," Obo said, hands on wide hips. The sun was high and sweat dotted his forehead.

Asha studied the ill-shaped wooden houses cramped

for space on the road. Chimney smoke poured from some of them. A few people wandered about on their morning errands, carrying bundles of straw, stacks of firewood, and squawking chickens in small cages. The smell of roasting meat rose on the air. Asha's mouth watered. Barefoot children whooped and cried, running after each other, playing games, and chasing goats. No one seemed to pay any mind to Asha and Obo.

After a moment they came to an inn. A sign above the door read *Matilda's*. A grin formed on Obo's face.

"Best banana beer for miles around," he said.

Asha made a sour face. She had never tried banana beer before, but it didn't sound too appetizing. Once, when Obo and some of the men were celebrating a birthday, she smelled his beer and almost gagged.

Obo pulled open the heavy door and they stepped inside. Asha coughed upon entering. The inn was smoky and loud. It was a long, low room with massive dark beams on the ceiling and blazing fireplaces on either end. Men and women sat at long tables eating and drinking. Some played a game on a checkered board, and others milled about doing nothing in particular. The room was full, taken up mostly by people with dark skin, like her and Obo and everyone else she had ever known. But mixed in with them were others with white skin and yellow, brown, or black hair. They were from Mercia, Asha realized.

Suna had told her about Mercia before. It was on the other side of the world, far from Alkebulan, where they had different gods and customs. Over time, though, Suna had said, people traveled far and wide, and some towns and countries were full of all types of people, living together in peace. *For the most part*, she had added with a grin.

A strong-looking woman with plump red cheeks and white hair tied back in a braid bustled through the crowd and approached them.

"Well bless me, if it's not Mr. Obo in the flesh," she said warmly. She gave Obo a huge hug and planted a wet kiss on his cheek. He swallowed, clearly uncomfortable at this display of affection in front of Asha. "Lady Matilda," he replied. "Please, meet my friend Asha."

Matilda leaned down and looked Asha in the eyes. "You don't look like one of his brood," she said, examining her as if she were a horse at auction.

"She's an orphan," said Obo protectively, "in my care."

Matilda raised an eyebrow and straightened back

up. "Hmmm," she murmured. "Never took you for the fatherly sort. No matter." And here she knelt down and pinched Asha so hard on the cheek she winced. Matilda laughed. "Well, any friend of yours is welcome. Come along now, let me find you something to fill your bellies."

Asha rubbed her cheek as Matilda led them through the crowded inn. Several people looked up from their mugs or plates to study them.

"Why are they looking at us?" she whispered.

"We're strangers," Obo replied over his shoulder. "Take no offense, Asha."

Still, she didn't like being stared at, stranger or not. Plus, her cheek hurt from Matilda's pinch.

Most of the tables were long and narrow, with people fighting for elbow space. Fortunately, Matilda led them to a small table in a back corner, away from the crowds.

"This should do just fine," Matilda said, ushering them to sit.

Asha and Obo sat down with heavy sighs. Asha thought Obo might break the chair because it was so small, and was relieved he didn't.

"Now," Matilda said. "Take a load off, and I'll be back."

Asha tried to smile as best she could.

Obo peered around. "Just like I remember it," he murmured.

"You've been here before?" Asha asked.

"Long ago," Obo replied.

Asha jumped as a young woman with flaming red hair and white skin with a smattering of freckles across her nose placed a bowl of kola nuts on the table. She stared in disbelief as the girl sauntered away. "Her hair," she whispered. "Did you see it? Red as a sunset!"

Obo grinned. "You're in the wide world now, girl."

Asha wondered what else she would see as she got farther from the world she knew. What, exactly, would she find? And where were they going? The Underground Kingdom? They had no idea where it even was.

Matilda brought a huge mug of banana beer for Obo and a glass of tamarind juice for Asha. She'd only had it once before and loved it. In just a few sips, she drained the glass and asked for another. She sat back and exhaled. It felt good to sit and drink, although the chair seat was hard and she would have liked a pillow.

A few minutes later, the woman with the red hair returned, bearing trays of food. Obo's eyes lit up.

"That should get you started," she said, placing plates and bowls on the table. A wonderful aroma filled Asha's nostrils.

"Why, thank you," Obo said.

"Yes. Thank you," Asha put in, still staring at the girl's hair.

"Lady Matilda says you're both special guests, eh?" she replied.

Asha's ears twitched. She had a strange accent, almost as odd as her hair.

Obo flushed again. "Ah, well, she's a generous woman, that one."

She laughed and headed back into the throng of customers.

"Well," Obo said, looking at Asha. "You hungry?"

Asha didn't need to reply.

There were bowls of sweet lentils, salted pumpkin seeds, roasted goat with bananas, eggplant in a hot simmering stew of mixed vegetables, and huge loaves of flat, brown bread. Asha ate so much she thought her stomach would burst.

"Ahh," sighed Obo contentedly, leaning back in his chair and clasping his fingers across his broad stomach.

"Burrrp!" Asha's hands flew up and covered her

mouth. "Oops," she said. "Sorry!"

"*BURRRPPP!*" Obo answered, a loud, deep belch emanating from his belly. They both laughed heartily, a slight reprieve from the terrors that had befallen them.

After they'd eaten their fill, Obo rose to catch up with Matilda at the front of the inn. Asha surveyed the room. Amid the bustling and noisy crowd, she noticed a boy, probably a few years younger than herself, staring in her direction. He wore no shirt and his brown pants ended in tatters below his knees. His skin was white, and lank, black hair hung to his shoulders. Asha absently fingered the rim of her glass as she returned his glance.

To her surprise, the boy got up from his seat. And he was headed her way.

Asha stiffened, suddenly on guard. They were in a strange place, among even stranger people. She raised her head, trying to get a glimpse of Obo up front but she didn't see him. She curled her hands into fists. The boy was standing in front of her in an instant.

"Wanna play?" he asked.

Asha eyed him warily. He was absolutely filthy.

"Play?" she asked. "Play what? Where?"

The boy looked left, then right, then picked up a checkered board and drawstring pouch from a nearby table. He moved aside Obo's empty plate and laid the items down, then upended the pouch. Several wooden pieces clattered onto the table.

"Draughts," he said.

Asha raised an eyebrow.

"Some people call it checkers," he said, taking Obo's seat across from her. Asha drew back a bit. She could see dirt around his neck and under his fingernails. His eyes were odd, like two black stones, and his chest was covered with what looked like bruises. He reminded her of a small bird that had fallen out of its nest.

"What's your name?" she asked.

"Sprix."

"Sprix?" Asha echoed back. An odd name, one she had never heard before.

"And you?" he asked, setting the checkers on the board.

"Asha."

"Asha," the boy said softly, as if weighing its meaning. "Okay, this is how you play draughts, Asha."

As Sprix showed her the rules of the game, she took the time to study him. He was young—even younger than she'd thought. He looked like he'd led a hard life. Dark circles were under his eyes and his face was sad, as if he had already seen too much of the world.

In no time, Asha found herself wrapped up in the game, which involved landing and capturing the other player's pieces. Finally, she spied Obo, leaning over the bar talking to Matilda. He gave a tilt of the head, curious, it seemed, as to what she was doing. With only a glance Asha let him know that everything was okay, then turned back to the game.

"I won!" she shouted.

Sprix crossed his thin arms and leaned back in his chair. He surveyed the board with intensity. "You're pretty good," he said. "For a girl."

Before Asha could tell him exactly what a girl *could* do, a man's shout rose over the din, and a figure in a mud-splattered brown cloak came striding up to their table. He was as big around as Obo, with a pockmarked, pale face and tufts of wispy orange hair on his head.

"There you are, you little urchin!" he growled, grabbing Sprix by the arm.

Asha drew back.

"Ow!" Sprix cried out as the man yanked him from his chair.

"Thought I told you to finish mucking out the stables!"

Sprix looked to Asha desperately, as if asking for help, but Asha didn't know what to do. Right at that moment, Obo appeared out of nowhere, a mug of banana beer in hand. "Ho, now," he boomed, taking in the scene, "unhand the child."

The man looked Obo up and down, gathering the measure of him. "Mind your own business, blackamoor! Out of my way!"

He shouldn't have said that, thought Asha.

The man tried to brush Obo aside, but as his arm swept out, Obo grabbed his hand and bent the fingers back.

"Aieee!" the man cried and buckled to the wooden floor. A crowd had gathered, talking and jostling for the best view.

"Now," Obo began, "is there anything else you'd like to say?"

The man grimaced, his face racked in a spasm of pain. "Unhand me, sir," he began, his voice suddenly contrite. "I only come for what's duly mine, see. He's my . . . son, and he's run off. Shirking his duties, as it were."

He had an unusual way of speaking, Asha noticed, with words she had never heard before. Obo still had the man's fingers in a vise, and his face was becoming a

shade of red Asha had never seen before. She imagined
Obo could snap them like dry twigs if he wished.

Obo looked at Sprix. "Is this man your papa, boy?"

Sprix stared at the floor. "Yes—yes, sir," he stam-
mered.

Obo released his grip. The man let out a grunt, stood
up, and shot Obo a look brimming with fear and anger
in equal parts. "With me, boy," he commanded, curling a
crooked finger at Sprix. "*Now!*"

Sprix meekly shuffled toward his father, who took
him by the ear and led him away. Just as they reached
the door, Sprix craned his neck around with much effort,
and gave Asha another pleading look. And then the door
banged shut behind them.

It took a few moments for the crowd to disperse, but
soon enough, they were once again shouting for more
food and drink. Asha and Obo sat across from each other
again. The game pieces had spilled onto the floor, and the
woman with red hair came and retrieved them, giving
Asha a small smile as she did so.

Asha felt terrible. "Can't we do something?" she
asked. "He's probably being beaten right now."

Obo looked Asha in the eyes. His bald head gleamed
with sweat and the silver ring through his nose glinted.

"I'm sorry, Asha, it's none of our concern. That man's his papa, see, the boy said so himself. There's no cause for us to come between them." He took a big gulp of beer.

Asha was crestfallen. "But he was terrible to him! Didn't you see! He beats him!"

Obo shook his head, then took another swig of beer. "I'm sorry, Asha. It's not our place to interfere when it comes to a person's family."

Asha knew Obo was right. There was nothing they could do. But she liked the boy for some strange reason. He'd seemed harmless enough, and only looking for a friend.

Obo stood up and stretched his massive arms over his head. "We best be getting some rest."

Asha yawned. It was still light out, but they were both dead tired. After their meal, she felt like she could fall asleep right there at the table.

Matilda showed them their rooms. Asha's was simple enough, but there was one thing there she'd never seen before. It was a wooden frame that rose up from the floor on four sturdy legs. Atop it, pillows and covers were gathered. It was a bed. A real bed. Asha sat on it first, testing her weight. Her life with the troupe meant that beds were usually on the ground, with several layers of linen and heavier blankets. Being a ward of Suna's, they had their own tent and, more importantly, privacy. But this felt different.

She lifted her legs onto the bed and lay back, studying the wooden beams of the ceiling. When she was little, she used to gaze at the clouds and, through the sheer power of imagination, will them into recognizable shapes: birds, tigers, elephants. But tonight, what she saw was much more ominous. Two dark, penetrating eyes. Staring . . . staring . . . staring.

SEVEN

THE BURNED TOWN

ASHA AWOKE TO THE CHIRPING of birds. Sunlight poured through the small window. She hesitated a moment before getting up, as it was the first time she'd ever slept so comfortably. What would it be like, she wondered, to live like this every day? She'd be spoiled, she knew that much, and never want to return to her old life.

She got up slowly at last, and walked to a washstand where a porcelain bowl was placed. A soft towel was draped across it. Asha lifted the cloth and dipped a finger into the water. It was warm. Someone—maybe the girl with red hair—had crept in to fill it while she slept. Asha wet a corner of the cloth and rubbed the sleep from her eyes. It felt good. She did the same with her neck and elbows. She basked in the moment, not knowing when she would get another chance like this during their travels. Reluctantly, she finally threw on her clothes and bounded down the rickety steps to the inn.

Obo, Matilda, and a few other locals were already seated for breakfast at a long common table. Matilda had laid out sweet potatoes, fried plantains, sliced mango, all types of grains in little bowls, and mugs of sweet goat's milk. Asha's mouth watered just looking at it all.

"Good morning, Asha," Matilda said. "Grab a plate. Better get it before Obo does."

Asha smiled and pulled out a chair to sit. She glanced at Obo, who looked as if he wanted to burp again.

"Sleep well, little one?" Matilda asked.

Asha scowled. She didn't like being called little, but she couldn't be rude.

"Yes. Thank you, Lady Matilda."

"My pleasure, sweetling," she replied.

Asha picked up a fork and dug in. She couldn't believe how lucky she was to enjoy another fine meal, although sitting with strangers made her a little anxious. But Obo didn't seem bothered, so she followed his lead.

"It's getting worse everywhere," a white man with a long black beard was saying. He had a face like a cat, made all the more strange by the abundance of hair on his face. "We heard of an attack a few nights back, a town just west of here. People dragged out of their homes in the middle of the night by masked men. Women and children, too. All taken to who knows where." He slammed his mug on the table for emphasis.

Asha shuddered. She shot a glance at Obo, whose eyes told her she should say nothing of the attack.

"The Shrike is searching," the man said. "For something. Or *someone*."

Asha almost spat out her milk. There was a hushed silence around the table, broken only by the mewling of a cat outside.

Even Obo paused in his eating.

"They say he has a tower," the stranger continued, "far away in the Burned Lands. And at the very top of that tower is a nest. The Shrike's Nest, where he takes his victims."

Asha felt as if the milk in her stomach had just curdled.

"Hmpf," a black man with ropy locks of hair scoffed.

"And how would you know? Ever seen this Shrike's Nest?"

Several heads nodded in agreement.

The man with the cat face chewed his food slowly. He took another swallow of his drink, then looked left and right, making sure everyone waited on his words. He had an audience now and was relishing it. He leaned forward and lowered his voice. "Some say, the people who were taken . . . knew *magic*."

Asha's intake of breath broke the silence.

"Magic?" Matilda sniffed. "If there was magic in this world, I'd be the first one to use it." She peered around the room with an air of exasperation. "I'd buy a new tavern, some fancy clothes, and put everyone to work so I could get some peace and quiet 'round here!"

The man smiled, but it was one of disdain, as if he were better than everyone else at the table. "Magic is real, woman. Used to be, at least. Long ago. No one remembers anymore."

Asha looked to Obo and thought of Suna. She had used magic, and so had Asha. At least, she thought she had. *How?* Would she be taken as well? Snatched in the night by shadow men?

Another uncomfortable moment of silence passed. Obo drained his glass and rose from his seat. "Well," he said, putting an end to the conversation, "we best be going." He thanked Matilda and nodded to Asha, an indication that she should follow him.

Asha rose and headed back up the stairs to gather her few belongings. The stranger's words rang in her ears: *The Shrike's Nest, where he takes his victims.*

Try as she might, she couldn't shake the troubling thoughts away.

Outside, the sky was a brilliant blue, and Asha could already feel the heat on the back of her neck. Matilda was kind enough to give them a small amount of food from her kitchen. It wasn't much, but it would help them survive for a while.

Matilda sighed as she looked at Obo. Asha realized how pretty the innkeeper truly was. Inside, the light was dim and yellow, and Asha hadn't really seen her beauty, but out in the bright sunshine her face was pleasing and her eyes twinkled.

The smell of horse and straw rose on the air. Asha watched a small boy kick a ball made of what looked like rope down the street. She thought of Sprix, and wondered if he was safe.

"You take care of this one," Matilda told her. "He's big enough, but not too bright now and then."

Obo gave her a look of feigned anger and then laid a hand on her shoulder. "Thank you, friend. I shall return the favor someday."

Matilda waved him away. "Just let me see your handsome face more than every three years. How about that?"

Obo swallowed loudly. Matilda stood on her tiptoes to give him a kiss on the cheek. Asha held back her giggles. Matilda sure knew how to make Obo uncomfortable.

They made their way through the town and onto the trail that had led them there. Once they were out of earshot, Asha turned to Obo. "Did you hear that man? He was talking about the Shrike. Why did he come after us?"

"Best to stay quiet for now," Obo replied. "And don't mention that name again." He peered around warily. "If he really does exist, he could have spies anywhere."

Asha wasn't looking forward to walking again, but they had no choice. *Why didn't Obo buy a few horses?* she wondered, although she had never ridden one before. And they surely must cost a lot of money, she reasoned.

Obo told Asha he had distant relatives not too far

away. There, they could rest again and figure out what to do. It was as good a plan as any other. As they walked, the blue sky shifted to a somber gray.

An hour after leaving the inn, they passed the smoking remains of a small town, where horses and dogs roamed freely, sniffing about for scraps of food. A row of fire-scorched houses stood against a dull, cloudless sky. There was not a soul to be seen.

"Where is everyone?" Asha asked, looking around. "Who burned this place?"

Obo didn't answer, only pointed.

Asha followed his finger. Up ahead, a curious symbol was burned into the wooden front door of a house: a bird's head in profile, sharp beak open in mid-cry. She stared for a long moment. Her head felt light on her shoulders. The image she saw when she read the tea leaves came racing back—a bird, with jet-black eyes.

"It's him," she said. "The Shrike. That man at Matilda's was right. They're taking people who know magic."

Obo shook his head. "We don't know that yet," he said, as if trying to dismiss the idea. But Asha could see in his eyes he was just as concerned as she was.

She peered around the ghostly landscape. A child's dolly lay at her feet, scorched and black, with the straw falling out. She saw that the symbol was burned into several other doors as well.

"How could someone be so evil?" she said angrily.

Obo sighed. "Come, Asha."

But Asha didn't move.

"Asha?" Obo persisted, concern spreading across his face.

"I need to find the Underground Kingdom," she said, as if in a trance. "That's what Suna said." She looked at Obo and her eyes welled up. "I . . . I don't know what it means. What am I to do?" She hung her head and began to sob.

Obo laid a hand on her shoulder. "You are not alone, Asha. I will not leave you."

His words were a comfort, but the desolate town stirred a stronger emotion, and it was one of fear.

They carried on and took refuge in a small clearing where a stream gurgled and splashed over jagged slabs of black stone. The gray sky faded and the sun was high and bright again. The warmth raised Asha's spirits, and they ate a little of the food from Matilda's supplies.

After another hour's march, Asha was tired once more. Her feet were sore and the pack on her back made her feel like a mule carrying its master's burdens. They finally made camp as the sky was darkening. Asha was relieved. She felt like she couldn't go any farther. A full moon slowly took shape in the sky.

Asha lay awake under a blanket of twinkling stars. The ground was hard and her lightly padded bedroll was little relief from the roots and sharp rocks that dug into her back. Lady Matilda's bed was sorely missed. Obo had risked a small fire that was now burning low. Thin wisps of smoke drifted up to become lost in the canopy above them. Asha's mind raced with thoughts of shrikes and shadow men. *What does it all mean? What is the Shrike doing? And what part do I play in all of it?*

Footsteps.

Asha bolted up.

Branches breaking.

Obo was up in an instant too, his knotty pine staff in one hand and his bullwhip in the other. "Stay quiet!" he whisper-shouted as he crept into the darkness.

Asha stood and glanced around in the dark. She wouldn't be caught without a weapon again. She scanned the ground and picked up a large broken branch, just big enough to raise a welt on an intruder's head. But what if it was the shadow men? A mere stick wouldn't help. She gripped it with both hands anyway, ready for whatever was coming.

She waited, nervous energy coursing through her body. *If it's a shadow man I'll kill him. I did it before and I can do it again . . .*

She gasped as two figures crashed through the trees.

EIGHT

A POEM OF OLD

N O! DON'T HURT ME, SIR!" a voice cried out. "Please!"

Asha stared in disbelief as Obo came into view holding a small boy by the scruff of his neck.

Sprix.

Obo released his grip and the boy hit the ground with a thud. A fresh purple bruise bloomed on his collarbone. He wore the same tattered pants as before and his feet were bare and dirty.

"What are you doing here?" Obo demanded.

Sprix's black eyes shifted back and forth between Obo

and Asha, terrified. "I followed you," he said quickly. "I've run away. Please . . . don't send me back. My pa . . . Finn. He beats me!"

Obo crossed his massive arms. "We don't need your papa coming after us, boy. We've enough trouble as it is. Best be on your way."

Sprix's eyes suddenly went watery. What little moonlight there was spread along the ground where he sat. "No," he said softly. "I . . . can't."

Obo raised an eyebrow. "What do you mean 'can't'?"

Sprix stared at the ground.

Asha felt pity for him, with his dirty clothes and skinny arms. "How did you get away?" she asked.

Sprix visibly swallowed. "I don't know. I just did."

"And how did you find us?" Asha pressed him. "You couldn't have followed us all this way without being seen."

"I don't know," he said again. "I'm just good at finding my way around the woods." He looked up. "Please don't send me back."

Asha turned to Obo and put on her best imploring look, the same one she had used when she was little and wanted a ride on his broad shoulders. Obo exhaled in exasperation. "I'm not gonna haul you back there, boy.

None of my concern. If you want to follow, so be it."

Sprix, still quaking, suddenly smiled. "Thank you, sir, thank you, lady. I promise I won't be any trouble."

"Good," Obo grunted. "But if you bring any unwanted attention, I'll—"

"He won't," Asha interrupted.

Sprix smiled again, and this time, Asha saw that he had little rows of sharpish teeth, like a fox or forest creature of some kind. *Odd*, she thought.

A moment of silence passed. A night bird's cries sounded in the trees above them.

"Are you hungry?" Asha finally asked.

Sprix didn't even have to answer, as Asha saw him lick his lips like a hungry wolf. She shared some of their dried fruit and meat and Sprix ate it eagerly, savoring each small bite.

Soon enough, the boy curled up and fell asleep on the hard ground, as if it were something he had done every day of his life.

Obo stared at him and shook his head. "That's my curse," he said.

"What?" Asha asked.

"Helping people. It doesn't always work out the way you think."

72

"It just means you're kind, Obo. Nothing wrong with helping people in need."

Obo smirked. "Exactly, but I've been burned before, helping people who didn't deserve it."

Asha didn't really understand Obo's hesitancy. "He looks harmless to me. Look at him, he's just a boy."

Obo shook his head again. "Nothing's ever just what it seems, child."

Asha peered at the sleeping figure of Sprix. *Just a boy*, she thought, *who needs a little help. That's all.*

There was a chill in the air the next morning, and the ground was damp. Asha rubbed sleep from her eyes and peered around. Much to her shock, Sprix was nowhere to be seen.

"What did I tell you?" Obo exclaimed. "I knew it! Check the bags, Asha. He may have stolen supplies."

Asha was sure Sprix hadn't stolen anything. There had to be an explanation as to where he was.

"Told you," Obo muttered, rummaging around in one of his canvas bags, his face set in a determined scowl. "You never can tell who you can trust. I had a feeling—"

Sprix walked out of the woods with two rabbits slung

on a stick over his shoulder. "Who wants breakfast?" he said with a grin.

Obo stared with an open mouth, and Asha couldn't help but give him an I-told-you-so smile. A few minutes later, the smell of roasting rabbit filled the air. It was the best Asha had ever tasted. The juice dripped down her chin as she ate.

Obo licked juice from his fingers and eyed Sprix warily. "First you slip away without a sound and then you come back with these two plump rabbits. Tell me, boy. How'd you manage that?"

Asha thought it funny that her friend was being suspicious at the same time he was stuffing his mouth.

Sprix didn't take the bait. "I told you I know my way around the woods, didn't I?"

"Hmpf," Obo snorted, taking another bite. He didn't seem too worried now, with his belly full, Asha thought.

The next hour took the chill off the air and the dew from the forest floor. The trio set out again to reach Obo's distant relatives.

And then what are we supposed to do? Asha wondered. She knew they needed to find the Underground Kingdom. And then . . . well, she wasn't so sure.

They marched on for a few hours, and while Asha

once again grew tired, Sprix seemed to have the stamina of a seasoned traveler. His steps were quiet, and Asha barely heard him beside her. She didn't want to pry, but she really wanted to know his story and how he came to be under the power of this man—Finn, he had called him. His father. But if he really was his father, why did he call him by his first name? *I'll ask him soon enough*, she thought. *Just give it a little time.*

Obo called an end to their day's journey as the sun began to dim. They set up camp near a small stand of quiver trees with thick branches and dense foliage. Asha started a small fire and they warmed up the last few bites of rabbit. She stared at Sprix as he ate with nimble fingers.

"So," she said. "You know your way around the woods, do you?"

Sprix sat cross-legged on the ground. He didn't look up, but nodded.

"Do you know of a place called the Underground Kingdom? Where the black flowers bloom?"

Obo drew in a disapproving breath, but Asha ignored him. They'd never get anywhere if they didn't ask questions.

Sprix picked up a twig and studied it. "Nope. Don't know about black flowers." He raised his eyes to meet hers. "But I heard something once about a kingdom underground."

Asha froze where she sat. She glanced at Obo, who only raised an eyebrow. "What did you hear?" she asked. "A story?"

"It's not a story. It's a song."

"Song?"

In answer, Sprix stood up, dusted himself off, and then, as if he were a pupil at school, folded his hands behind his back and started to sing softly:

> *"Beyond the forest bright and green*
> *the clans of Aziza did dwell.*
> *The Baobab Circle, Ivy Grove,*
> *and Chestnut Clan as well.*
> *Spirits of Tree, Spirits of Wood,*
> *their magic deep and strong.*
> *But mortal ways and evil men*
> *into their land wrought wrong.*
>
> *"Search for the baobab, tall and strong*
> *for there you shall find their home.*
> *A kingdom, now underground . . ."*

Sprix trailed off and mumbled to himself. "That's all I remember."

Asha sat still, shock etched on her face.

Aziza. The strange word in Suna's book.

"Where did you learn this? Who taught it to you?"

Sprix sat back down. "I don't know. Only know the song."

"What do you mean you don't know?" Asha went on, her voice taking on an edge. "You had to learn it somewhere."

Sprix squirmed, clearly uncomfortable. "I just remember it from a long time ago. I don't know from where." He looked up, dark eyes shining. "Honest."

Asha turned to Obo and then back to Sprix. "We have to find this place, Sprix. It's important. Do you know where it is?"

Sprix wiped his nose with the back of his hand. "No."

Asha let out a labored breath. No one spoke for what seemed like minutes. Small animals scuttled in the surrounding forest. Asha had felt a peculiar sensation when Sprix sang the song. She couldn't quite put her finger on it, but it was like a longing for a land she had never seen before. In her mind's eye she saw great trees of every shape, some with gnarled branches reaching toward the heavens, and others that bloomed with white flowers and red berries. A fragrant aroma rose in her nostrils. All this was sensed in seconds, scenes from another world, beautiful and dazzling.

She eyed Sprix curiously. "These people. The Aziza. They still exist?"

Sprix shrugged. "Don't know, but—"

"But what?" Asha said, no longer being gentle. "What do you want to say?"

Sprix didn't seem to notice her impatience. "I once heard a story about the Aziza."

Asha closed her eyes and opened them again. She heard Obo shift where he sat on the ground. Asha gave Sprix a moment. He seemed like a fragile boy and she didn't want to cause him any more distress.

"It was a lady who told me," Sprix said. "With long, white hair and nice eyes. She told me that the Aziza can be found where the baobab grows." He paused for a moment, as if unsure whether to go on. "One time she showed me a drawing of a baobab. It was a giant tree that reached all the way up to the sky." He raised his small arms in the air.

Obo shook his head. *"Trees?* What will trees tell us?"

But Asha knew what it meant.

She turned around and pulled up her shirt just enough to reveal her mark.

"Asha!" Obo cried. But she stood with her back to them, moonlight casting a silvery glow upon her brown skin. "Did it look like this?" she asked.

Sprix drew closer and peered at Asha's back.

"That's it," he said, surprise in his voice. "That's a baobab tree. Your mark is a sign of the Aziza people."

NINE

NIGHT VISITOR

B Y THE FIVE," OBO EXCLAIMED. He had never
seen Asha's mark before and the surprise showed in
his eyes.

"That's a baobab tree," Sprix said again. "You're
marked by the Aziza."

Asha pulled her shirt back down and turned around.
The only sound other than the crackling fire was that of a
hooting owl. They all sat quietly. Asha rummaged in her
pack until she found Suna's book. She flipped through
the pages. There it was—the word *Aziza*—and the figure

with dark hair and penetrating eyes.

"If Asha bears this mark," Obo said, "she must have some connection to these people. Maybe that's what Suna meant."

"Who's Suna?" asked Sprix.

Asha told him about Suna and that she had died. An *attack*, was all she said.

"I'm sorry," Sprix said softly.

Asha nodded and gave a weak smile.

"So," Obo continued, stirring the faintly glowing coals. "If we find where the baobab tree grows, we may begin to get some answers."

Asha's stomach was tied in a knot. Her mark was a sign of the Aziza. What did that mean? What did the Aziza and the Underground Kingdom have to do with her?

A memory suddenly came back to her.

"Suna once told me that the baobab tree grows in the Dry Lands to the east. I remember now."

"That's many a mile from here," Obo said. "It would take weeks to reach."

"But we have to try," Asha said. "I . . . I have to figure out what all of this means. My mark . . ." She shook her head in frustration.

▲ ▼ ▲

Obo continued to lead them west to find his relatives. Night had fallen after another day's march, but there was no decision on whether they should try to reach the Dry Lands. They were in the opposite direction of where they were headed. Asha didn't know what they should do. How could they possibly make it that far east? They didn't have enough food and weren't even sure where the Dry Lands were.

"Perhaps the light of day will help us see things more clearly," Obo said. "For now, we should get some rest."

Obo was right, Asha knew. She was fatigued, and with Sprix's arrival and his song, her mind was going in all directions. But she had to sleep. She lay down and drew her blanket back up over her. Sprix curled himself into a ball and laid his head on the hard ground. "Here," Asha said, drawing off her blanket and giving it to him. "I have another in my pack."

Sprix looked as if he had just received a pouch of gold. "Thank you, lady," he said, wrapping it around his shoulders.

Asha smiled. "It's Asha, remember?"

"Asha, then," Sprix said. "Thank you, Asha."

The last coals grew cold as the three companions drifted off to sleep.

Asha dreamt that night. Visions of dark tunnels and small, fierce faces; of giant trees with limbs soaring to the heavens, and countless other images that drifted in and out of her sleep.

Lastly came the eyes, almond-shaped and slow-blinking. Dark, dark eyes that seemed to pierce her very soul.

Asha awoke from her dreams suddenly. The air was cold now that the fire had dwindled. Her eyes adjusted to the dark around her. Obo was snoring softly, his back against a tree, pine staff across his knees. *So much for keeping watch*, she thought. Then again, her friend must have been as tired and frightened as she was. *Should we really go east?* Asha wondered.

A sound like leaves being trampled nearby pierced the still night.

Asha sat up.

Before she even had a chance to alert Obo, a cloaked figure stepped from the woods.

A cowled hood covered the stranger's face. Obo was

up in a moment, his staff gripped in both hands. "Halt!" he cried out. Sprix leapt to his feet, quick as a fox.

The figure stepped closer and threw back its hood.

Asha gasped.

It was Suna who stood before her, returned from the dead.

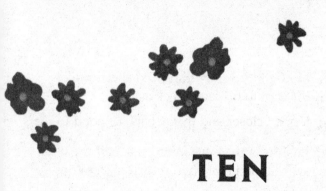

TEN

INYANGA

"B Y THE FIVE," whispered Obo.

"Suna?" Asha asked tentatively, her voice almost a whisper.

"No, child," the stranger said, "I am not Suna. But I am one of her sisters. I am Rima, and I am here to help you."

Asha shook her head, as if she were still asleep and trying to wake. The mysterious newcomer looked so much like Suna it hurt. She carried a spear with a long shaft ending in a leaf-shaped blade, and a weather-stained cloak was wrapped around her shoulders.

Obo still held his staff tightly and eyed the stranger warily.

"I mean you no harm, Obo," Rima said. "Suna told me of your friendship with Asha. Word reached me of the attack. I have been searching for you for days."

Obo didn't reply, only continued to stare.

Rima studied them both. "I am sorry for your loss. Especially you, Asha. I know Suna was like a mother to you." She laid a hand on her heart for a moment as if paying respect.

"Are you a witch?"

The voice was small and quiet. Asha looked left, then right. It was Sprix, she realized. She had almost forgotten that he was there with them.

Rima's eyes found Sprix in the dark. She tilted her head and studied him. "No, child. I am not a witch, but I do know a few."

Sprix smiled.

"Sister?" Asha ventured, a note of doubt in her voice. "Suna never said she had a sister."

Rima smiled weakly. "A sister not by blood, Asha, but by another bond."

"What bond?" Asha asked.

Rima eased out a breath. "I will tell you all, Asha,

soon. But now I must rest."

"Do you know what is happening?" Asha pressed her. "Why were we attacked?"

Rima moved closer and the light of the moon cast a glow on her features. Her kohl-rimmed eyes were just like Suna's.

"There is much to discuss, but I dare not speak here. The enemy has many spies. We must take council elsewhere. Get some sleep. All of you. I will keep watch."

Obo snorted. "And why would I trust you to keep watch, woman? You could be a thief in the night for all we know." He looked to Asha for agreement but she shook her head. Rima raised an eyebrow, as if someone speaking to her in such a manner was a rare thing. Asha understood his hesitation, but she didn't feel the same way. Even though the woman's answers were vague, she knew she wasn't a threat. There was something about her, aside from her resemblance to Suna, that gave Asha comfort. "It's all right, Obo," she said.

Rima gave a slight nod. Still, Obo held his pine staff at the ready.

Rima stepped closer and took a pack from her back. She spread a soft blanket onto the ground and sat.

"I'm afraid we don't have any food left," Asha said.

"Thank you, child, for your hospitality. I am fine. Rest is all I need at the moment."

"Rest, then," Asha said.

Obo watched the stranger with wary eyes. Asha did, too, but she also felt a small flicker of hope bloom in her heart.

Asha drifted in and out of sleep. She was too wound up by Rima's arrival. Why had Suna never told her about this sister-bond? What was Rima's story? Where did she come from?

Asha knew she was a friend. She just felt it. Maybe it was her eyes. Eyes like Suna's. Asha's mind was full of questions.

She drifted off again, and when she finally rose from her blankets, Sprix was roasting plantains on the fire. "Come eat," he said. "I climbed a tree and got these. They're ripe. There's enough for everyone!"

Sure enough, Asha saw that Obo and Rima were already eating the warm fruit. Asha rubbed the sleep from her eyes and groggily accepted Sprix's offering. She sat beside Obo, who looked just as unsure of Rima as he had the night before. As for their new visitor, in the light of day, Asha saw just how much she looked like Suna. They even had the same mark. Like Suna, she was graced with a wisdom knot, but hers was on the back of her right hand.

"My home is not too far," Rima said. "We can rest there, and I will tell you what I know."

Asha's ears perked up. *Answers. At last.* A moment passed where no one spoke. The sun was strong and birdsong sounded through the trees. Asha looked to Obo and gave a half smile. She then turned to Rima. "The Underground Kingdom. Where the black flowers bloom. Do you know what that means?"

Obo paused in his eating.

Rima held Asha's gaze. "I will tell you what I can, Asha, but I don't have all the answers."

Asha smiled. *Well,* she thought. *That's something, at least.*

Rima led the way, with Asha and Sprix behind her and Obo in the rear. They had been walking for an hour and Asha wondered about the spies Rima had mentioned. Were there shrikes perched in the highest boughs of the trees watching them? Or were they unseen creeping things she couldn't even imagine?

They crossed a number of dry ravines, then entered a deeper, thicker part of the forest, where black boughs reached down toward them like the groping arms of strange beasts. The only sounds Asha heard were her own footsteps and the soft swishing of Rima's cloak as she led them forward. Asha felt as if she were in a foggy dream.

"What is this wood?" she asked, her voice sounding strange in the silent forest.

"It is called the miombo," Rima replied. "It is old beyond belief. We do not have much farther to go. Come. Let us quicken our pace."

Asha peered up at the dense foliage overhead. The branches and leaves were so thick hardly any sunlight could reach the forest floor. After several turns and twists on the trail, they made their way out of the forest, and followed a stream until a simple stone house with a blackened chimney came into view. A well with a bucket hanging by a rope was to their left. A few chickens puttered around, scratching at the dry ground. A tree stump for splitting wood was next to a small garden with leafy vegetables.

"Home," Asha heard Sprix whisper. "A real home."

"Don't count your chickens yet," Obo said with a sour grimace.

Asha shook Obo's doubting words away and watched as Rima took a key from a leather band around her neck and opened the door. Asha jumped back, startled, as a flock of birds on the roof took to the air with a raucous cry. She shivered, reminded of the shrikes who had turned into men.

"Welcome to my home," said Rima humbly.

Inside, the house was cold and dark. Asha rubbed her arms and shivered at the absence of sun. Rima lit a few candles and then a fire in the hearth, and the space was soon filled with warmth. A lone table surrounded by four crude wooden chairs sat in the center of the room. Leather-bound books and a few clay mugs sat atop it. Like the outside of the house, the walls were of cold white stone. Jars of herbs and small bundles wrapped in cloth sat on a shelf, along with colored beads, pieces of wood, and what looked to Asha like the bleached skull of some strange animal. Asha took a deep breath. An odd mix of melancholia and happiness flooded her senses. Her eyes watered. The rich smell of herbs and undiscovered secrets reminded her of home.

Rima invited them to sit. The chairs were small, and Obo looked like a giant as he took a seat.

"I'll fetch water for tea," Rima said. "Make yourselves

at home." She took a pot from the table and headed outside.

Obo watched her departure and immediately looked to Asha when the door banged shut. "I don't trust her," he whispered.

"I think she's nice," Sprix put in.

Obo shot him a warning glance.

"She's all we have right now," Asha said. "If she was a friend of Suna's, she's a friend of ours."

"But how do we know?" Obo shot back. "How do we know she is truly a—"

The door creaked open and Rima returned. Obo went silent and stared at his boots.

Rima hung the pot by its handle on a bar over the fire, which was now crackling and hissing.

Sprix got up and sat with his legs crossed in front of the flames. Asha saw the firelight catch his eyes, which seemed to shift between brown and green.

"That should warm us up a little," Rima said. She walked from the hearth to the wall and picked up a jar from one of the shelves. "I'm afraid I don't have any food of substance, but these nuts and berries might stave off your hunger a bit." She handed a few to Sprix, who took some and passed the rest on to Asha, who in turn offered some to Obo, who only grunted and shook his head.

Rima fetched cups and poured tea. She sat with Asha and Obo while Sprix continued to stare into the flames as if under a spell.

Asha cupped her hands around the clay cup. An earthy aroma rose up in her nostrils. She took a small sip. Warm spiciness flooded her mouth.

Obo sniffed the tea apprehensively. Asha could tell he wasn't sure he liked this dark house and this strange woman. Finally, he spoke, a wary edge to his voice. "How do you know Suna?"

Rima sipped her tea a moment before she replied. "She was one of my people. We are sisters of a sort. We are of the Inyanga."

"Inyanga," Asha whispered.

"We all bear the same mark, the wisdom knot, and share much, much more. Do not worry, Obo. I am no enemy."

Obo relaxed his shoulders a bit.

Asha heard the cries of birds outside, as if they had all flocked back to the roof and were listening.

"Suna was known to many," Rima continued, "and the world is poorer for her loss." She paused. "We heard word among our kind of the Shrike's attack."

Asha stiffened. "Why? Why did he attack us?"

Rima sipped her tea again, her face expressionless. Obo shifted in his seat and gazed at her, as if wondering what secrets she held.

"Not long ago," Rima began, "Suna sent me a hawk with tidings. She had many questions. All about you." Rima's intense eyes pierced straight through Asha. "You were of great concern to her. She knew you were special, and she was beginning to understand that you are a force of great power."

Asha started, taken aback. "Power? What power? I'm just a girl. I don't have any powers." But she remembered the words she'd shouted. Words that had turned a black shadow into ash. *Back to the darkness.*

Silence fell on the room. Asha looked to the fire to see Sprix, now curled up and asleep.

"Asha," Rima said kindly. "Please, forgive my forwardness, but . . . may I see your mark?"

Obo gasped. "Asha. You don't have—"

"I know," Asha cut him off. "It's okay, Obo."

She scooted her chair back and rose from the table, then turned around and lifted her shirt.

Rima leaned forward in her chair and let out a breath. "Remarkable," she whispered.

"But what does it mean?" Obo almost hissed, impatience rising in his voice. "We need answers!"

"I cannot be the one to tell Asha of her fate. Only the Aziza can do that. It is not my place."

Asha lowered her shirt and turned around. "So, they're real then," she said. "The Aziza. The people from long ago."

"Yes," Rima answered.

Asha exhaled. The world she knew was slowly changing: shrikes and shadow men and an ancient race of long-lost people. What other wonders existed? *So it's all true. But what do I have to do with them?*

"The Underground Kingdom," she said, coming back to herself. "Where the black flowers bloom. Is that where they are? Can you lead us there?"

Rima's lips tightened. She tapped a ringed finger on the wooden table. "There is a way," she said. "But the paths are dangerous."

Obo sat up in his chair, puffing out his expansive chest. "I've walked into danger before. It won't be the first time."

Asha smiled.

Rima eyed Obo. "I promised Suna I would do all in my power to help protect Asha. I not only do this for her, but for all of us. The enemy is a threat that cannot go unchallenged." She stood up and drew closer to Obo, who rose to face her. Sprix stirred from the fire and knuckled his eyes. Rima did not back down from Obo's massive frame. "By the honor of the Inyanga, I swear allegiance to Asha," she declared. "By life or death, I will protect her."

Obo held Rima's gaze, then finally looked away. Begrudgingly, he nodded.

"Let us rest here tonight," Rima said, stepping away from Obo, the tension now broken. "Tomorrow, we will begin."

Obo slept outside—to keep watch, he said—while Asha and Sprix took their rest on the hard floor of Rima's home. Once again, Asha longed for the comfort of the bed at Matilda's inn. She wondered if she would ever sleep in a place like that again.

Sprix stirred beside her.

"Asha?" he whispered.

Asha looked to Sprix and then at Rima, sleeping peacefully on thin blankets across the room. Asha nodded to Sprix, a sign for him to go on.

Sprix propped himself up on his skinny elbows and

the low firelight caught his large eyes.

"The big one," Sprix said. "Obo. He won't send me back, will he? To Finn? He's probably looking for me right now."

Asha almost chuckled. "No, Sprix. He won't. He's not bad. Just kind of grumpy sometimes."

Sprix gave a half smile.

"Why does he treat you the way he does?" Asha asked. "Your father? You call him Finn. Why?"

Sprix sat up a little more, pulling the blanket tightly around him. He opened his mouth but then closed it. "He's . . . not really my—"

Sprix stopped short as Rima rolled over and sat up. "What is it?" she asked, alarmed. "Is Obo keeping watch?"

"Yes," Asha replied. "Everything's fine. We were just talking."

Rima blew out a breath. "Get some rest," she told them. "Tomorrow will be a long day."

"Yes," Asha replied. "We will."

She looked to Sprix once more, but he was already rolled up in his blanket again. He was slowly beginning to let his guard down, Asha realized. *I need to know his story*, she thought. *And I'm going to get it.*

Asha awoke with a crick in her neck and a cramp in her leg. She sat up awkwardly, trying her best not to make it worse. The pleasant aroma of toasted bread put her aches out of mind, if only for a moment.

"We'll need a little something to eat before we set out," Rima said, turning a slice of toast over the fire with tongs. "The village is nearby. I left early to buy bread while you slept."

The door creaked open and Obo appeared, looking as if he had seen better nights.

"Good morning," Rima greeted him.

Obo grunted and gave a solemn nod.

They gathered around the table and shared toast and tea. The bread was so good Asha wanted more, but there was none to be had. Sprix pressed his finger to the table and picked up every last crumb. Afterward, Rima lit a candle and cupped her hands over the small yellow flame. A thin black wisp of smoke rose to the ceiling, then disappeared. She closed her eyes and began to whisper. The words were too quiet for Asha to fully hear, but she watched Rima's lips move, her brow furrowed in concentration.

Rima's eyes flashed open. "Hold hands," she said urgently. "All of you."

Asha took Obo's large, calloused hand in hers and

held Sprix's in the other. Once all were joined, Rima closed her eyes again and murmured a few more words. The small flame went from yellow to white, and then to a deep bloodred, which flickered and sputtered in the stone room. It seemed to grow in size and its shadow loomed on the wall, a black shape slowly waving back and forth. When it appeared to almost fill the room, Asha flinched back from the table, and the flame went out, as if a silent breeze had stirred the air.

"What was that?" asked Obo, looking at Rima. "What have you done?"

Rima released a labored sigh, as if she had just spent a lot of energy. "It is a small spell of protection. There are many dangers in the world, Obo. This may give us a little help. Come, we should leave now. There will be less danger by daylight."

Asha watched as Rima opened a black woven bag and placed the small wrapped bundles from the shelf into it. She dampened the fire and led them out of the house and back into the forest. The house had been warm, but the sun still felt good on Asha's neck, and after a few minutes, her aches and cramps had disappeared.

They took the same trail that had led to Rima's house, but veered east when it split. After a few moments of walking, Asha spoke. "Are we going to the Underground Kingdom? How will we get there?"

Rima didn't look at her as she answered. "By the will of the Five."

She pulled her hood over her head.

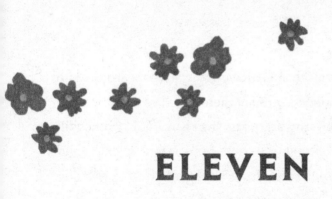

ELEVEN

TORU

RIMA LED THEM through deep forests to a range of mountains called the Gahinga—great peaks that formed a jagged outline against a red sky. The first few days and nights of travel were uneventful. Food was scarce, and Rima foraged for edible plants, which she then boiled and turned into a kind of soup, adding herbs and spices from her bag. Sprix caught a few rabbits. Asha had no idea how he did it, but he often wandered off without her even noticing, only to return a short time later with a plump bounty. *Strange*, thought Asha. She noticed Rima studying him with curiosity as well.

Slowly, they began to feel more and more at ease with one another, and soon, Asha came to experience the same sense of familiarity and trust with Rima as she had with Suna. Even Obo reluctantly became less suspicious, and now and again he and Rima would huddle and talk quietly together, and she would tell him of the roads they would take.

Asha still wanted to know more about Sprix, but she had yet to find the right moment. One evening, Rima drew her aside. "He is holding a secret," she whispered, nodding to the boy asleep by the fire.

"A secret?" Asha repeated. "What kind of secret?"

"I don't think he means you harm, but there is a veil around him, one I cannot pierce."

Asha eyed Sprix in the firelight, her curiosity growing stronger by the moment.

Long days turned into quiet nights, and Asha felt as if she were walking in a waking dream. Every day was the same. Walk. Rest. Eat. Sleep. One night, as they sat quietly around a small fire, Asha asked Rima about the Inyanga.

"Some would call us witches," Rima replied. "But in truth, we are a much older and ancient race. There are not many of us left who still use the Old Ways."

"What are the Old Ways?"

"We harness the power of earth, air, fire, and water, but only for the cause of good. It takes a great evil to stir us to act, and I am afraid that time is now upon us."

Asha remembered how Suna had called wind from the sky to push back the shadow men. She looked into the fire, focusing on a branch slowly turning to ash. "When we were attacked," she said, staring into the flames, "before Suna was killed, I felt this . . . power, running through my body. I yelled some words that I didn't know."

Rima remained silent, waiting.

"I shouted, 'Back to the darkness,' and then this . . . shadow monster died. How did I do that?"

Rima sat on the ground, her cloak spread over her shoulders. It was the same color as Suna's—black, with threads of red and gold. Obo sat with his back against a tree, listening intently, while trying to appear as if he wasn't.

"There are many mysteries in the world, child. And you are one of them. I do not have the answers, Asha, but I think the Aziza will."

Asha shook her head and stared into the fire. *Mystery?* she thought. *Me?* But deep down inside she knew she was different. How could she not be, after what she had already seen and done? *Back to the darkness,* she thought. There had to be answers.

Soon, she fell asleep, along with the rest of her companions, but the questions still lingered.

Asha awoke with a start, her heart racing.

Although the night was cold, drops of sweat beaded her brow. Obo was standing watch and the embers of the fire were burning low. Asha thought that the forest suddenly felt different somehow. It closed in around them, dense and heavy, the air itself fraught with some unknown presence. Rima stirred from sleep as well and joined Obo and Asha by the fire. Sprix sat up and hugged his blanket around him.

"Something is astir," Rima said warily. "I feel a presence." She peered deeper into the forest, her eyes taking in the surrounding darkness. "It is old . . . whatever it is."

"I feel something, too," Asha put in. And although she couldn't say exactly what it was, she could certainly sense it, deep inside her spirit.

Obo picked up his whip from the ground. Rima laid a hand on his shoulder. "Careful," she whispered.

"Whatever this is, we do not want to disturb it. There are many things in this world of which we do not know."

Obo snorted. "Anything that tries to come into this camp will be met with a crack of thunder."

A rustling in the trees behind them made Asha and the others turn.

"Look," Asha said, pointing. "There's something there."

Two small green lights wavered and bobbed in the forest. They seemed to be floating, as if they belonged to someone . . . or some*thing*. Every now and then they would wink out, only to reappear again after a few seconds. Now the lights were moving again, and they were coming toward the camp. Rima stood silently, her eyes scanning the darkness.

Asha didn't hear a sound.

Then, as the group looked on in amazement, something stepped out of the forest.

It was a gazelle, Asha saw, but unlike any she had ever seen before. Its eyes were curiously aware, a deep, luminous green filled with light and—it seemed—wisdom. *A gazelle's eyes?* she wondered, thinking back to the floating lights.

Its coat gleamed red, slashed with streaks of black.

Two silver horns flared back from its graceful head.

"By the Five," Obo whispered.

Rima approached the creature warily. "Toru," she said, bowing. "Great Forest Father."

"Hail, Lady Inyanga," the gazelle answered.

Asha felt unsteady on her feet. The gazelle had just *spoken*. Obo remained still, frozen. Sprix stared in wide-eyed wonder.

"I sensed you in the forest," Toru said. "I am glad to see that your kind still walks among us."

"There are too few of us left," Rima said, "but we will do what we can against the evil that has arisen."

Here the gazelle—Toru, Rima had called him—rumbled deep in his throat. His eyes shone even brighter, and Asha thought she saw a flickering flame in their depths.

"The Shrike!" Toru bellowed. "He is burning and killing! We have seen his birds on our borders, gathering in great numbers. They are searching"—he turned his head to gaze at Asha—"for someone."

Asha swallowed hard. She felt as if every part of her being was exposed, her innermost hopes and fears laid out to look upon. The gazelle stepped forward and stood close to her. Asha's legs shook, and she felt trickles of sweat on her back. To her surprise, Toru lowered his head and sniffed about her. "There is great power here," he said, "ancient power."

Asha remained frozen, not from fear but sheer awe. *Ancient power?* She smelled damp earth and smokiness around the gazelle. There were other smells, too: clove, cinnamon, and something that she could not place, but was familiar all the same.

"She is marked with a sign of the Aziza," Rima said. "We seek the Underground Kingdom. Only there will we find answers."

Toru stepped away from Asha and looked at each of them for a long moment. Lastly his gaze rested on Rima. "What you seek is now hidden from the world, Inyanga."

"Still," Rima replied, "we shall search."

Toru snorted again and stamped his hoof. "My folk are not far from here," he said. "Come. Follow my light."

And then, with his head held high, horns shining silver in the night, he bounded off into the deep woods.

TWELVE

A GOLDEN THREAD

THEY QUICKLY BROKE CAMP and followed Toru. "Gazelles," Obo said, as if in a daze. "Talking gazelles. This world is much stranger than I thought, Asha."

Asha couldn't believe it either, but still, she had heard Toru—*a gazelle* with the power of human speech. She shook her head. Rima and Sprix were in front of her, following Toru, while she and Obo took up the rear. *"Great Forest Father,"* Rima had called the creature. A ghostly shimmer seemed to radiate from him, like silver moonlight. Asha quickened her pace, as he and Rima were moving quickly. Sprix skipped and hopped, as if this were all a game of some sort.

Toru led them to a clearing ringed by a grove of giant moringa trees. The sky above was a net of glowing stars. Grass and verdant moss sprung under Asha's feet. She heard the splash and gurgle of water passing over stones and turned to see a small stream to her left.

Toru lifted his head and sniffed the air. "Rasha!" he boomed. "Ossia!" Asha jumped from the sheer power of his voice. A rustling in the forest made her turn. Two more gazelles appeared out of the wood. They were both as huge as Toru, with eyes just as fierce. The one to his right was a lighter shade of red, with silver antlers, while the other possessed a coat that was a deep, rich brown. White antlers stood proudly upon its head. Asha thought she would collapse from the sheer magnificence of it all.

"Hail, Toru," one of the gazelles said, and Asha felt as if the voice came from the ground she stood upon—a rumbling so deep it coursed through her whole body.

Although the night was pitch-black, Rasha and Ossia seemed to cast their own light, just like Toru, and there was no need of a fire.

"Here is Rima," began Toru, "one who practices the Old Ways, a mistress of the Inyanga. With her is the human child Asha and her companions. They seek the Underground Kingdom, and our old friends, the Aziza."

Asha looked on silently. The wind stirred the top branches of the surrounding trees. It was as if every living thing in the forest had stopped their nightly wanderings to watch and listen.

To Asha's surprise, Rima stepped forward, bowed her head, and then raised it. "Great Toru," she started. "We did not know we were close to your domain. Indeed, I'd thought you and your kind might have passed from this world, but I am glad to see I was wrong."

Toru rumbled, and a snort of steam escaped from his nostrils.

"I would ask," Rima continued, "that you help us in this hour of our need. We must travel far, and safely. I would ask that you let us travel the Golden Path." She paused, and Asha could feel her nervousness as surely as she felt the cool air that suddenly stirred around them. "Will you light the way?"

Asha stared in wonderment. Somehow, these creatures were the protectors of a path of some sort. If it helped them get to the Underground Kingdom more quickly, she was all for it.

She continued to stare at the gazelles—she tried not

to, but couldn't help herself. They were extraordinary. Their large eyes landed on her with curiosity, solemn and intelligent.

Toru turned his head toward Asha. Once again, she felt as if he was inside her mind, reading her thoughts, which made her uncomfortable. She focused on the earth under her feet, the wind in the trees above, and the rippling sound of water nearby.

A high-pitched barking suddenly rang in her ears. For a moment, Asha thought another animal was on the move in the forest, but as she looked and listened more closely, she saw that the gazelles were speaking to each other in a language Asha had never heard before. She looked to Obo, who could not hide his amazement.

This went on for several minutes until Toru finally faced Rima. The forest was silent again, and the only sound was Asha's own heartbeat pounding in her ears.

"It has been many an age since mortals have walked the path," Toru said. "Only those found to be true of heart and purpose may do so."

"I vouch for my companions," Rima said. Asha saw Obo bristle for a moment. "Asha is a foundling, raised by one of my sisters. She is important, and has a part to play, but we do not know what it is. Only the Aziza can help us, if we can find them."

A part to play? Asha thought.

"I make my own choices," Obo said, taking two steps forward. Asha closed her eyes. *Obo! What are you doing!*

Obo looked to Rima and then Asha. Asha felt tension in the air. "And I choose to stand with Asha . . . and Rima."

Asha sighed a breath of relief.

"Asha is . . . family to me," Obo went on, "and I will not see her come to harm."

Asha blinked back tears. The barest hint of a smile graced Rima's face.

"I will help, too," said Sprix, who had been standing next to Asha, quiet as a mouse. Asha hesitantly laid a hand on the small boy's shoulder and he looked up, his eyes like two pools.

"What say you, Asha?" Toru asked.

Asha looked from Sprix to Toru. She swallowed as every eye fell on her. Her mouth was dry. She wasn't sure what she was about to say, but the words came out anyway. "Thank you, Great Forest Father," she said, the same way Rima had. She stopped for a moment and looked at the ground. She felt as if she might cry, but she willed herself not to in the presence of these strange and wonderful creatures.

She raised her head higher. "I know there is something I am meant to do," she said, "but I don't know what it is. But I will do what I can to stop the Shrike."

Obo smiled proudly. Toru remained silent. He continued to peer at Asha, and once again she felt as if the great gazelle was inside her head, reading her thoughts.

"We will light the way," he finally said.

Asha heard Rima's sigh of relief the same time she felt her own.

Toru stepped away from her and formed a circle with Rasha and Ossia. They began to stamp the forest floor with their hooves, like a dog would do as it digs in the dirt. The air was charged with some sort of energy. Asha felt the fine hairs on the back of her neck rise.

Abruptly, flickers of light ran along the ground and traveled up the gazelles' sleek bodies. A flash pulsed between Toru's antlers, blinking faster and faster until it became a whirring ball. Toru dipped his head and the ball danced between Rasha's antlers, then Ossia's. They were passing it between them, each one adding more and more energy, the air colored by sparks of green, red, and blue. The ground trembled under Asha's feet. A light blazed in the forest, suddenly turning the dark night to day. Asha gasped and threw her hand up in front of her face, but when she drew it away, night had returned, and she saw a golden thread weaving its way along the ground like a spider's web, to become lost in the deeper part of the forest.

"Take the Golden Path," Toru said. "Do not stray from the light. There are other forces that work to destroy it. May the blessing of the Royal Lioness go with you."

"Come," Rima said, taking Asha's hand hurriedly. Asha clasped it. Sprix and Obo stood behind them.

"Remember," Toru said. "Do not stray from the path." He looked to Asha. "We will meet again, child."

Asha wondered when that would be.

Then Rima took a step forward, and Asha followed.

THIRTEEN

THE BURNING BRANCH

I T WASN'T REALLY A PATH, Asha realized as they followed the golden thread that wove its way along the forest floor to points unseen. At least not the type of path she was used to. From time to time, it winked out and reappeared again a few hundred feet away. Asha thought she could actually feel it leading her, a warm glow that started at her feet and rose to the top of her head.

They were still in the same forest where they'd met Toru and the gazelles, but the colors were more vibrant now, even in the dark. The green leaves, the small yellow flowers under their feet, it all seemed so much more alive. Asha thought she caught the faint sound of music somewhere on the air, but she wasn't certain.

Obo looked around warily. "Talking gazelles," he said flatly. "By the Five. No one will ever believe it."

Asha shook her head. "But we'll know. That's all that matters."

Obo nodded, but his face still showed his disbelief. Asha knew how strange it was, but she accepted it. What else could she do?

"Thank you," she said to Obo.

Obo cocked his head. "For what?"

"For saying what you did. That we were family."

Obo waved her away. "Of course, you are, child. Of course, you are."

They walked in silence for a few minutes, following the golden thread that weaved its way along the ground.

"Obo?" Asha said. "How did you meet Suna?"

Obo exhaled a deep breath. "Ah," he said. "Have I not told you this before?"

"No," Asha said. "You never did."

"Well," Obo started. "My home was called Enkolia. We were at war with another country, Domi, for many years. I was a soldier, Asha."

"So, you fought," Asha replied, "and . . . killed people?"

"I am not proud of it, but yes. I have killed. We were attacked. We had to defend ourselves."

Asha wondered if she should keep asking questions. Obo never talked about his past and she didn't want to lose the opportunity to learn more.

"But you said you were enslaved," Asha went on hesitantly. "How . . . how did you get away?"

"Our enemies defeated us and Enkolia was destroyed. I was taken as a slave, and held captive for years, until the people of Saba, a neighboring country, came to our aid. When I returned to Enkolia, my home was destroyed and everyone I once knew was gone. Years later, I met Suna when she came to my village. She invited me to join her troupe. She gave me a new home, Asha . . . and a family."

Asha was stricken. She had no idea of Obo's true past. "Thank you for telling me, Obo," she said. "You are my family, too." She risked a quick glance at her friend, and thought she saw his eyes glisten.

The golden ribbon snaked ahead of them; every now and then little diamond-shaped stars winked within its depths. Asha couldn't take her eyes away from it. She realized that she wasn't thirsty or hungry, though it had been a while since they had eaten. "How is this possible?" she asked Rima. "Talking gazelles and this golden path?"

"The world holds many mysterious secrets, Asha. Not all are fortunate enough to see them. Many years ago, it was said that the Royal Lioness created paths for mortals to travel quickly from one place to another in times of great need. And the Gazella are the protectors of it."

"Gazella," Asha said. "So that's what they're called?"

"They have many names," Rima replied. "In other lands they are known as the Erarak and the Maghrebi."

"How does it work?" Asha asked. "The paths? Is it magic?" The word seemed to echo throughout the forest and drift back down through the branches.

"*Magic* is a word people use for things they do not understand," Rima said with an edge to her voice. That was something Suna would have said, Asha realized. She didn't mind it one bit.

Sprix came up behind Asha, his steps quiet. They didn't speak for a long time, only followed the golden line ahead of them. Unseen night birds in the trees above them hopped from branch to branch, squeaking and chirping. Asha thought of Rima's warning: *He is holding a secret.*

"Sprix," she started, her voice low. "You said that . . . Finn wasn't really your father. Who is he, then? Where are you from?"

Sprix bit his lip. He was struggling with how to answer, Asha could see that clearly. "I'm not sure," he finally said.

"Not sure?" Asha repeated. "How can you not know where you're from?"

Sprix hesitated again before speaking. "I don't remember," he said with finality, and Asha knew he didn't want to say more. *Maybe it's too painful for him to talk about,* she thought. *I should just let him be.*

"I'm sorry, Sprix," she said. "I know you're still frightened of him. But if you ever want to talk about it, I'm here. You can trust me."

Sprix turned to Asha, about to speak, but the ribbon of light they had been following abruptly winked out, leaving the group in darkness.

"Stay close together!" Rima whispered.

Asha peered around nervously. The absence of the light made the forest not only darker but much more ominous. Every creak of branches made her stiffen.

A sound began to rise in her ears. It was a buzzing, like the bees she had seen working at a honeycomb once when she was with Suna. But this was deeper, and much stranger.

Obo reached for his whip. Rima held her spear at the ready. The buzzing grew louder. The moon appeared from behind the clouds, spreading a little light. The droning sound filled the forest around them, but they couldn't tell from where it came. Asha had to stop herself from clamping her hands over her ears. The night birds she'd heard earlier were now shrieking, disturbing the uppermost branches. "What is it?" she cried out.

"There!" Obo pointed.

Asha whipped her head to the left. The golden thread was visible again, though its light was faint, which gave them all a chance to see what was approaching. Asha's heart leapt to her throat. A swarm of creatures, wings outstretched and flying low, rushed toward them, breaking branches as they advanced.

They looked to be dragonflies of some sort, with multicolored wings. But that was not the most striking thing. As they drew closer, the buzzing sound increased and Asha saw small, wiry beings astride them, with sharp points at their elbows and knees. Before she even had a chance to cry out, the swarm was upon them.

Obo swung his whip in a circle above his head, connecting with one, now two, sending the creatures spiraling out of the air, wings flapping and buzzing. Asha didn't know what to do. Once again, she had no weapon.

"Behind me!" Rima shouted, as she raised her spear

in the air, its leaf-shaped blade glinting in the moonlight. She twirled it faster than Asha thought possible, both arms raised above her head, sending the strange attackers crashing into the surrounding trees. But with their mounts now destroyed, the riders rose up and charged on foot.

"Sprix!" Asha shouted, whipping her head left and then right, searching. *Where is he?*

The small figures attacked fiercely—climbing trees and then leaping down onto them, or running along the ground to attack from below. Asha kicked out, trying to stop them from getting any closer. She felt like she needed a broom to sweep them all away.

"Back!" Obo shouted as he cracked his whip, coming to Asha's aid. One of the dragonflies charged at Rima and she smacked it aside with a gloved hand. Asha got a clear look at its rider as it fell to the ground. It was human-faced, but with a mouth full of sharp, crooked teeth. Its clothes were some sort of spiky armor, which made her think of a beetle. She turned away in disgust, glad she had not been bitten by one of the ghoulish things.

A commotion to her right made her turn. Something large was moving through the forest. And quickly.

Asha gasped as a huge beast crashed through the trees. She shrunk back at the same time she recognized what it was—a great black horse, nostrils flaring, throwing up dirt in its path. It reared up on its hind legs and then came down, crushing and stomping. Asha saw huge muscles flexing beneath a lustrous coat.

She turned from the horse to see one of the winged enemies coming straight toward her. She looked around for a weapon and spied a thick branch at her feet. *Quickly!* she screamed inside her head as she snatched it up. She swung not a moment too soon, sending the thing and its rider into a tree. But she didn't have time to marvel at what she had just done. The horse was still kicking out and rearing up, its teeth drawn back over its gums, its eyes wild and fierce as it continued to fend off the attackers.

"To me!" Rima called, and Asha and Obo rallied to her side again. The horse, strangely, seemed to heed Rima's call as well and knickered quietly. A foamy lather glistened on its coat.

"There's something else here," Rima whispered. "Something—"

She was cut short as a thing made from nightmares appeared from the forest.

Asha shivered.

Walking slowly, as if it feared neither man nor beast, came a human-shaped thing covered in thick, black hair.

Barrel-chested, it stood on cloven hooves, and its head was that of a hyena. Its eyes glowed bloodred.

"By the Five," whispered Obo.

Asha trembled as the beast drew closer. Much to her horror, the monster opened its gruesome mouth and spoke. "The girl. Give her freely and my master will be kind. Refuse, and your suffering will last into eternity."

The horse stamped its hoof, ready to charge.

"You will not come near her!" Rima said, her face set in a hard scowl. "Not while I live!"

"Nor me!" Obo cried out, curling his whip around his wrist.

The beast charged with a roar, its steps thundering on the forest floor. Asha sprung back. She had heard hyenas before, and this was similar, but tinged with what she thought was a human voice.

Obo struck out with his whip, tangling it around the thing's cloven hooves. The horse stamped and circled it, as if looking for an opportunity to attack.

Asha needed to do something to help. She looked down at her hand to see that she still held the branch. She raised it up. "Back!" she shouted.

At that moment, power seemed to swell inside her. She felt it coursing through her body, through her arms and legs and every hair on her head.

"Back!" she shouted again, and this time, the branch burst into flame.

The foul monster stumbled on its hooves, as if afraid.

"Go back to the darkness!" Asha cried, waving the burning branch. "Go away, foul Butrungin!"

She swung the branch at the same time Obo lashed out again with his whip. The black horse found its opening and reared back on its hind legs and kicked the thing in its chest. It fell back, grimacing.

"You have no power here!" Rima cried out. "These paths are for the light, not the dark!"

She raised her spear to the heavens. A streak of lightning blazed down through the trees and struck the creature dead.

All was silent.

Obo was breathing hard, bent over with hands on knees. Rima stood tense and alert, searching the forest with those fierce eyes of hers. Asha still held the branch, its flame now spent.

The mysterious horse shook its great mane and snorted. Asha approached it warily, but it only folded its legs and settled to the ground. Sweat slicked its coat. Asha tentatively reached out a hand.

"Careful," Rima warned.

Asha touched the horse on its head. She looked into its eyes, eyes she had seen before, two pools of inky black.

"Sprix?" she asked.

FOURTEEN

STRANGERS

LONG, MISTY TENDRILS suddenly swirled around the horse's body. Asha couldn't tell if they were coming from the ground or the horse itself. Rima knelt and looked closer. "Impossible," she whispered.

Asha stared in awe as the mist became a heavy blanket of fog, completely covering the animal, and then slowly fading to reveal another form: a boy. Sprix.

"A shape-shifter," Rima hissed, standing up. "I knew he had a secret."

"Gods be with us," Obo whispered.

Asha's mind was reeling. She hadn't had time to think

about the burning branch, or the bizarre monster they had just defeated. She reached into her pack and found a tattered blanket, which she drew over Sprix, who was unclothed. *How can it be?*

Sprix stirred and opened his eyes.

"Here," Asha said, helping him to sit up.

"Water," he croaked. Asha reached for her pouch and handed it to him. He drank greedily, his throat working desperately.

"That's enough," Rima said, not too kindly.

Sprix set the pouch on the ground and wiped his mouth with the back of his hand.

"Why didn't you tell us of your gift before?" Rima challenged him.

Sprix looked up, pupils still wide, just like the black horse's. "Gift?" he said. "I think it's a curse."

"A curse?" Asha repeated.

"Finn said it was. Said I was left by a faerie and they took his real son."

"A *faerie* shape-shifter, then," Rima said. "A rare combination, indeed."

Asha felt like Rima and Sprix were speaking another language, one she had no idea how to understand. "What . . . is a faerie?" she asked.

"A creature not wholly human," Rima replied. I have heard tales of these folk living on the far side of the world in Mercia, but they are something not known in this land."

Asha was still breathing hard from the attack and having trouble gathering her thoughts. Sprix wrapped the blanket around his skinny shoulders and looked at her. He was a boy again. Just a boy in the woods.

"Why didn't you tell me?" she asked.

Sprix stared at the ground. He seemed at a loss for words. "I thought it was safer to keep it a secret." He sniffed. "I'm sorry, Asha."

Rima eyed Sprix with a questioning gaze but said nothing.

"I just wish you would have told me," Asha said.

"What were those things?" Obo asked.

"Minions of the Shrike!" Rima spat out.

Asha looked at one of them, dead, inches away from where she stood. It was terrible to see. The wings were beautiful, a kaleidoscope of luminous colors, but its rider was something entirely opposite: it had a small human-like body, lank black hair, and sharp teeth.

"And the other thing?" Obo put in. "The demon?" He looked to Asha with the same expression on his face as when she'd turned the shadow men into dust.

"You named him, Asha," Rima said. "Butrungin. How?"

"I don't know," Asha said in a quiet voice.

"And the branch?" Rima pressed her.

Asha shrugged, speechless, trying to form words. "I just felt this . . . power. I held it up and it was on fire!"

Rima gave a wry half smile. "It seems Toru was right. You are indeed a source of great power, wouldn't you agree?"

Asha exhaled. *I did that. I made fire out of thin air.*

"We must keep moving," Rima said at last, turning and looking ahead of her. "We can't be too far now."

Asha still had so many questions, but with a sigh, she followed Rima.

They continued along, following the glowing ribbon. It felt to Asha as if they had walked for hours. Her mind was dizzy with everything she had seen. The world was stranger than she could have ever imagined. She had turned a branch into flame. How? And the beast. Butrungin. How did she know its name? Sprix's revelations were also bewildering. A shape-shifting faerie?

"We will rest here tonight," Rima suddenly announced, interrupting Asha's thoughts. They made their camp under a small stand of trees with long, droopy limbs, their leaves providing shelter of a sort. Once they were settled in, Obo fell fast asleep. Asha and Sprix lay on their backs, gazing up at the night sky. Rima tended a small, crackling fire. "A horse," Asha said flatly. "How is that even possible?"

Sprix stirred next to her. "I've always been this way. It feels normal to me."

"Why didn't you run away before this?" she asked. "You could have turned into a horse and run for your life."

Sprix's eyes shined wetly in the dark. "I was scared. Finn said if I ever did, he would hunt me down and . . . kill me."

Asha felt for the boy. He had been so terrified and mistreated he couldn't even imagine running away.

"What did he . . . make you do?" Asha asked. She hoped she wasn't being too nosy, but she needed to know.

Sprix shook his head slightly, as if trying to shake away a memory. "He made me work. In the stables and around his house. He beat me."

Asha reached out for his hand. Sprix squeezed it and looked at her. "People paid him money to see me change. Into my . . . other self. He made me do it."

"I'm sorry, Sprix. That's terrible."

They sat in silence a moment, the only sounds Obo's

heavy snores and the crackling flames. Asha suspected that Rima heard every word she and Sprix shared, even though she was several feet away, tending the fire.

"Tell me a happy memory," Asha said, shifting on the ground, trying to change the mood. "You have to remember at least one."

A crooked smile spread on Sprix's face. "My mum and me. She used to pick flowers and—"

He stopped short as a sound came from the forest nearby.

Rima turned from the fire, peering into the dark. Asha heard movement and rustling in the trees. The moon, which had been cloaked by clouds, suddenly cast a pale light over the camp. "Obo," she whisper-shouted.

Obo groaned and sat up. "What is it?"

The answer was revealed as three shadowy figures slowly emerged from the woods. Rima rose and hefted her spear.

Asha stared. She was frozen. Was this a dream? She blinked, but the three figures remained in her sight.

"By the Five," Obo whispered.

The strangers stood only as tall as Asha, but what they lacked in height, they made up for in their presence, for they were fierce and proud, and seemed poised for danger at any moment. They were bare-chested and brown-skinned, with strange markings that ran up the length of their arms. Their hair was long and black as night, woven into braids that fell to their shoulders. Curiously, they wore trousers like a child would, cut just below the knee. Small bows were slung across their backs with full quivers, and daggers hung from their belts. Rima held up her free hand in greeting. "I am Rima of the Inyanga," she said, bowing.

One of the warriors stepped forward.

Asha looked upon him in wonder.

He was small, but she saw strength coiled in his body that seemed ready to unwind at any second. His eyes were like a cat's, almond-shaped and slow-blinking, as if his heart beat in some strange rhythm, unlike those of humans. He stared at her with intensity.

I've seen those eyes, Asha realized. *In my dreams.*

Asha couldn't hold his gaze for long. It was too . . . intense. His skin was as worn as old leather, and the marks running up his arms took on a multitude of patterns: stars, interlocked circles, wings, and other symbols she did not recognize.

"I am called Pulligan," he said. His voice was deep and rich, which was strange to Asha, coming from such a small body. "This is Acanthus and Ohen." He nodded in the direction of the two others who accompanied him. "We are Aziza of the Baobab Circle."

Asha's mouth opened in awe and surprise. She turned to Obo, who raised his eyebrows.

"We heard of your coming from our friends in the forest, the Gazella," Pulligan went on, "for we still speak the language of the wind, unheard by humans." His eyes landed on Rima. "You would never have found our kingdom if we had not sought you out, for even the Inyanga cannot see paths that are not there."

Pulligan smiled, and it seemed odd, as if smiling were something he was not used to doing.

He fixed his eyes on Asha. She wanted to turn away, but she couldn't. Her feet felt as if they were rooted to the ground. But as she stood there, unmoving, she heard a voice that said: *We seek the child who is foretold in prophecy. By my dreams she has been revealed.*

Pulligan drew closer to her. His eyes, the same fathomless eyes she had seen in her mind's eye, seemed to peer into her soul. She saw timelessness there, generations of sadness, love, and hope. She was afraid, because Pulligan would not avert his gaze.

"Many have come before who would hold claim to the prophecy," he said, in an almost threatening tone, continuing to peer at Asha. She swallowed. Obo slowly reached for his whip. In a flash, Acanthus drew his bow and nocked an arrow, aimed right at Obo.

Rima broke the tension. "She has been marked," she cautioned, holding up a hand. "Show them, Asha. Do not fear."

Asha, shaking, hesitated. She let out a long, stifled breath and stepped back a few paces. She turned away from the onlookers and hitched up her vest and undershirt. Asha heard the patter of small feet and then felt eyes on her back. A bird flew across the round orb of the moon. After a moment, she drew her clothing back down and turned around.

Pulligan stared at her. His companions, Acanthus and Ohen, eyed her anew, their faces nearly masking their surprise.

"The first sign is true," Pulligan said, holding out his arms, "for she is marked with the Mother Tree. We must return to the kingdom. Only then can we prepare for what must come."

Asha watched as at least two dozen Aziza, spears in hand, their faces noble and ancient, stepped out of the forest to join their leader.

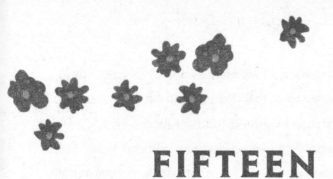

FIFTEEN

A DOOR OF STONE

ASHA AND THE OTHERS FOLLOWED the Aziza into the forest. It took a moment for her to realize that the Golden Path had winked out. She supposed that meant they were now safe. At least she hoped so.

Pulligan and his companions made hardly a sound as they marched through the woods. Some carried spears with leaf-shaped blades, and others bows and arrows. Asha and her friends were hemmed in, with the Aziza ahead of them and behind. It almost felt like they were prisoners, Asha thought, but she was sure they were doing it for their own safety.

Their movements were fluid and graceful, and although they stood only as tall as children, their angular faces were marked by deep brown lines and crow's feet. *How old are they?* Asha wondered. She couldn't believe it. The Aziza, the people Suna had written about, here in the forest leading them . . . where?

And what did they have to do with her? *The Mother Tree*, Pulligan had said, and *The first sign is true.* Asha's head spun at the sudden turn of events.

The Aziza led them through the forest over many twists and turns, and Asha felt as if they were going in circles. Sprix walked warily, as if afraid of the strange people. The trees became more dense and closed in around them, blocking the light of the full moon. Finally, they came to a clearing where a stone wall loomed up before them. Two great trees stood on either side, their branches curving down to frame the wall. Asha watched as Pulligan laid the palm of his hand upon the stone surface. He turned to face Asha. "Never before have we led outsiders into our realm. Once you enter, you are sworn to the Aziza." He eyed each of them fiercely. "If you betray our trust, you will meet a swift death."

Asha trembled at his words, but inside her head, she thought: *Just you try it.*

"We are sworn to Asha," said Rima without hesitation. "We will not betray you."

Obo nodded, but he clearly did not like Pulligan's words, either. Sprix gulped, and it seemed that Pulligan finally noticed him. He cocked his head like a curious cat and stared at Sprix, unblinking. "Hmm," he murmured, after a long moment, and then turned away.

A low whispering began that rose to a chant. Asha looked around and realized it was coming from the Aziza, a humming drone of sorts. There were words but she did not understand them. They were singing, or chanting, a melody that was strangely familiar. It lifted on the night air and rose into the trees overhead to become lost in the wind. Pulligan kept his palm on the stone wall as the voices continued their chorus. Then he lifted his hand. Asha gasped as the wall vanished.

She was in total darkness. She stretched out her arm in front of her and spread her fingers, but felt nothing. In the distance, she heard the drip of water. Obviously, some sort of Aziza magic had taken place, because one minute she was standing outside the stone wall and the next, they were inside this place.

Pulligan spoke a word that she knew meant *light*, even though she had never heard it before. The space suddenly brightened. Not the brightness of daylight, but a dim, yellow glow, just enough to see by. Asha looked around and found her companions right next to her.

She was relieved to finally get a sense of where she was. They were in a cavernous room, with torches affixed to the red walls. It was a cave of some sort. Dark passageways leading to who knew where forked left and right of her. She looked up to see that there was another level above, with rope bridges spanning the distance. The flickering glow of small fires could be seen. "Follow me," said Pulligan.

The light was brighter now as Pulligan led them through a maze of tunnels. Asha realized that she wouldn't be able to make her way back to the entrance if her life depended on it. The air was dense but not cloying, and full of a fragrance she couldn't place. It was sweet like berries, mixed with woodsmoke, cloves, and a scent that made her head feel light on her shoulders. The ground below her feet was soft earth, scattered with small branches and flat stones. As they walked, she felt hundreds of fierce eyes focused on her. Obo, Rima, and Sprix were quiet, but Asha noticed their apprehension.

They turned into another tunnel. It was narrow, and they all had to walk single file. Asha didn't like tight spaces. She heard Obo breathing heavily behind her. Just as she was about to feel faint, they exited into another broad area, and Asha gasped in wonder.

They were standing in a large open area with a roof high above. Birds flew overhead. But that was not what took her breath away.

"Behold the Mother Tree!" Pulligan announced, his arms held wide in praise.

Asha craned her neck up. The giant baobab tree towered above her, soaring toward the small patch of light that shone from an opening in the cavernous roof. The trunk was massive, wide and mighty, with thick, gnarled branches. At the very top, clumps of green leaves were bunched together.

"By the Five," Obo exclaimed.

Pulligan spoke again. "The Mother Tree has been with us for generations. For a thousand years it has stood, through battle, peace, and turmoil. It is written that it will one day bring forth blooms, flowers such as never seen before." He turned to face Asha. "Lay your hand upon the tree."

Asha stood still. She looked to Obo, who only exhaled through his nostrils and raised an eyebrow, a silent gesture of uncertainty. But Rima's gaze was different. It was almost a smile, and a light shone in her eyes that reminded Asha of Suna. Sprix nudged Asha with a sharp elbow. "Do it!" he whispered.

Asha let out a breath. *This is where Suna told me to come. This is what I've been searching for.*

She took a step forward. Small wooden bowls filled with water were placed around the tree as if in offering. She reached out with her right hand and, with trembling fingers, placed her palm on the rough bark of the trunk.

Asha soared over lush, green forests and silver ribbons of water. She was a great bird, and the currents of the air lifted her higher and higher into a brilliant blue sky, the breeze like silk on her feathers.

She winced as a sharp pain shot through her. She began to fall. Her head grew dizzy. She was struck. An arrow had pierced her side. Drops of red blood fell to earth, where they bloomed into trees that sprouted red berries.

The vision quickly passed, but another came before she could even speak out.

Tribes of Aziza, dressed for war, stood before a great army on a desolate plain. Asha heard the brash clamor of horns and the whizzing of arrows by her ears. Aziza warriors fell in a heap, their small bodies pierced.

Asha gasped, and her eyes flew open. But in an instant, she was transported again.

A small person—creature?—with a mask of feathers around the eyes sat on a throne of bones. "Asha," a voice called. "It is time. We will meet soon."

Suna peered out from a veil of darkness, her eyes deep and true as ever. "Your time has come, child. You are stronger than you know."

What sounded like a drum beating inside her head brought Asha back to the moment. She had removed her hand from the tree but she didn't remember doing it. A tingling current ran through her whole body, as if she'd been struck by lightning. She had seen visions—glimpses of things she didn't understand. But she had seen Suna, too, and her words were a comfort to her.

She heard a gasp and turned to see Obo and Rima peering skyward. Asha raised her head.

Flowers were falling from above.

But they weren't just any flowers. They were a deep purple, so deep it was almost black. Asha stooped and picked one up from the ground. She turned it over in her hand. "Where the black flowers bloom," she whispered aloud.

Pulligan raised his arms in the air again. "Behold! The empress is come! Asha! She Who Brings Light!"

Asha stood frozen as the small group of Aziza laid down their weapons and knelt at her feet.

SIXTEEN

THE TALE OF AMIRA & SAKA

A SHA STOOD STILL BEFORE THE great tree, speechless. A slight breeze caressed her face, though the outside world felt far from this strange place.

Empress? she thought.

Black petals were strewn around her feet and the thick, brown roots that forked from the base of the tree spread out like limbs. As if in a waking dream, she felt Pulligan lead her and the others away from the Mother Tree into a clearing where woven mats of leaves and grass were offered for them to sit upon. An Aziza man set down soft pillows to make a special place for Asha.

Sprix, Obo, and Rima sat down nearby, after Asha had been seated. Obo's face was a study in bewilderment.

"How can this be?" Asha asked quietly. "Rima, what is happening?"

"It seems that you are indeed the one of which the prophecy speaks, Asha."

"But what is the prophecy? Why me?"

Rima didn't answer, but cast her gaze toward Pulligan, who turned to Asha. For a moment, she thought he wasn't going to answer, but finally, he spoke, his eyes fixed on her. "First, we must visit the past, Empress, for there you will find answers."

"I'm not an empress," Asha said sharply.

Pulligan smiled his odd smile. "In time, you will know, Empress."

Asha shook her head in confusion. Everything felt slow and dreamy, as if she were asleep: the graceful movements of the Aziza, the slowly falling petals, the sound of a drum beating in the distance. Asha's world had turned upside down yet again.

Pulligan shifted on the seat of woven grass. "Listen," he said, "for the past is where we find truth."

And then he began his tale.

"Many years ago, after the great war, what remained

of our kind fled underground, to the deep woods and forgotten caves of this world, and humankind and Aziza did not meet for any reason.

"But one morning, a young Aziza woman named Amira was gathering fruit from the marula tree. She loved to sing, and on this day, her voice carried throughout the forest until it reached the ears of a human man named Saka, walking nearby.

"He followed the sound and came upon her without warning. Amira was shocked and ran away in fright. She realized that she had strayed too far, and had found herself near the domain of humans. But before Amira fled, she saw the man's eyes, and thought him to be kind.

"Many moons passed until, once again, Amira visited the forest, singing as she walked among the flowering trees. To her surprise, she heard another voice accompanying hers. Who could it be, she wondered, who knew the songs of her people?

"She followed the melody until she came upon the man she had seen before, but this time, she did not flee. They spoke to one another, and he told her how he loved the music of the Aziza and wished that they had never been at war. They stayed in the forest until the sun melted behind brown hills and night birds began to sing. This was the beginning of their love for one another."

Asha smiled. It was a nice story, but she wondered what it had to do with her. She tried not to let her impatience show as Pulligan continued.

"In time, they were discovered, for they met in secret. My kind did not approve of such a love, nor his, so Amira fled the kingdom."

"Where did they go?" Asha asked, entranced.

"There are a few places in Alkebulan where people are left to their own ways, Empress. They found one such place, a small village. And there they lived in peace and began a family.

"They had a son, and they called him Adisa. He favored his mother, that side of him that was Aziza, and was made fun of for being different. He was quick and wary like a bird, so children began to call him Bird Face and Little Wing, because children can be cruel. They knew of his parents, and thought it unnatural for someone like him to be born into their world. One day, he thought, he would get his revenge.

"During his thirteenth summer, a group of older boys mocked him relentlessly. They chirped and squawked whenever he was near. They challenged him to fly away from the rocks they threw. But one day, as Adisa fled into the woods to escape their taunts, he stumbled upon a dead bird lying at the foot of a quiver tree. He was mesmerized by its beautiful wings, iridescent in the sunlight. He realized that a bird was a thing of beauty, not something to be laughed at."

Asha felt a sudden awareness, as did her companions, that something more than a mere folktale was being laid out for them. Something . . . *extraordinary*.

"This gave Adisa an idea. He would shape a mask of this bird, and he would wear it proudly as a tribute to these magnificent creatures that graced the heavens. But he also wanted revenge and power, so he would never be mocked again.

"It was then that Adisa met in the woods a powerful sorcerer called Bazaal. The sorcerer asked him why he was so angry with the world and Adisa told him of how he was teased because he was half Aziza. Bazaal saw this as an opportunity to incite hatred in Adisa, for he was cunning and evil, and used people for his own gain. He instilled in him a hatred of the Aziza people so fierce that Adisa's blood boiled. He told him that it was the Aziza who made him this way. The side of him he thought weak and ugly was all their doing.

Asha leaned in, focused now. She couldn't have turned away even if she had wanted to.

"Bazaal promised him strength and power he could never imagine, if only he would give him his spirit, his very essence, for Bazaal was more than just a sorcerer. He was a demon who lived on the souls of others.

"Adisa agreed to relinquish his soul, for he thought that it meant nothing. From that day on, Bazaal gifted him with power beyond ordinary mortals, and he grew strong and cunning. He called himself the Shrike in tribute to the mask he wore upon his head."

"The Shrike?" Obo said, and then sheepishly brought a hand to his mouth as if he had spoken out of turn. Asha was entranced by Pulligan's tale, learning about the Shrike and where he came from. But still, what did it have to do with her?

Pulligan paused and sipped from a wooden cup. He took his time doing so, and Asha watched as he swallowed. He set the cup back down, cleared his throat, and continued.

"Through dark magic, Bazaal crafted black armor for Adisa and he became terrible to look upon. Adisa's new-found strength was a joy to him, and he made a vow to destroy what was left of the Aziza people, for it was *they* who had made him weak. He fled his home and moved to a desolate part of the world—the Burned Lands, the site of a great battle many years ago, between men and our kind.

"He built a tower and called it the Shrike's Nest. And he began to search the world for the Aziza and imprison them, all because he hated who he was."

"But this is all about the Shrike," Asha finally said. "What does it have to do with me? And this . . . prophecy?"

All was silent.

Asha looked around at her companions. Some of the Aziza avoided her glance when she tried to catch their eye. *What is happening?* she thought.

"Empress," Pulligan said, and his gaze was fierce. "The Shrike. He is your brother."

SEVENTEEN

SECRETS REVEALED

ASHA WONDERED if she was asleep and only dreaming. There was no other explanation for how this could be happening. Her head felt heavy on her neck.

The Shrike. My brother?

Rima, Obo, and Sprix looked on as Asha sorted through her feelings in front of everyone.

"Twelve years after Adisa left home," Pulligan said softly, "his parents had another child. That child was you."

Asha licked her lips. Her mouth was as dry as old twigs. "Amira," she whispered, looking into her lap.

"Saka. My mother and father." And then, the full enormity of it finally struck home, and she raised her head. "If . . . Adisa was half Aziza, that must mean that . . ."

"Yes," Pulligan said, answering the question she hadn't fully asked. "Our prophecy tells of a child, half human, half Aziza, who will be marked by the baobab. She will unite our tribes and lead us into battle . . . against the Shrike. That child is you."

Obo sucked in a loud breath. Rima looked on proudly.

Asha's heart leapt to her throat. "Battle? Me?"

"In our tongue you are named Empress," Pulligan declared. "She Who Brings Light."

Sprix smiled enthusiastically. "I knew you were special," he said softly.

"Where are they?" Asha asked. "My parents? Are they . . . ?"

Pulligan let out a long breath. "I believe that when the Shrike learned of the prophecy, he sent his spies to every corner of Alkebulan, searching for Aziza. He scoured every village and town, every place he thought we were hidden." He paused. "In the end, Empress, we believe his spies found your parents. I am sorry."

Asha's chest heaved. "But they are alive? Please tell me they are alive!"

She didn't mean to raise her voice, or let the tears come, but she couldn't help it.

"I truly do not know, Empress," Pulligan replied. "But I am sorry to say . . . they may have passed from this world."

Asha refused to accept Pulligan's answer. "But you don't know, do you?" she said, her voice continuing to rise. "You have no proof!"

Rima reached over and laid a hand on Asha's shoulder.

Pulligan looked into Asha's eyes. "No, Empress. We do not have proof. Anything is possible."

Asha tried to focus and wiped the tears away from her face. She had only just learned of her parents and now they had been snatched away from her, a cruel turn of events. "But what happened to *me*?" she asked. "Why wasn't I taken?"

"That, I can answer," Rima suddenly spoke up.

"What?" Asha said, turning away from Pulligan. "What do you know?"

Rima looked abashed, and her dark eyes softened. "I was sworn to secrecy, Asha. I only learned of it days before Suna died."

Asha felt as if she had been pierced by needles. No

one had been truthful with her. *No one!*

"What did Suna tell you?" she asked flatly.

Rima sighed and clasped her hands in her lap. "The night that your mother and father were taken by the Shrike's forces, Suna and her masquerade were camped in the same town. Your mother knew of Suna, and she often visited the masquerade to listen to the tales that the griots spun.

"One night, Suna heard a cry for help, coming from your parents' home. She and some of the others rushed there to find your mother and father fending off an attack. They were being overwhelmed by the Shrike's spies. They all fought bravely, and even some of the neighbors tried to help, but in the end your mother and father were taken. You were thrust into Suna's arms and she took you. From that day forward, Suna cared for you."

Asha shook her head. This was all too much. She swallowed, trying to calm her breathing. "Did you know this?" she asked Obo.

"No . . . Asha. This was before I met Suna. I am sorry I was not there to protect them."

"Why didn't Suna ever tell me?" Asha demanded. "That my parents were alive? That they fought to protect me?"

"I do not know . . . Empress," Rima answered.

"I'm not an empress!" Asha shouted.

Her outburst echoed throughout the cave. Rima low-ered her head a moment, as if in apology.

"You will come to understand, Empress," Pulligan said softly. "In time."

Asha closed her eyes and opened them again. She would never get used to being called empress, no matter how often they said it.

"The Shrike is gathering his forces," Pulligan said. "He is searching for you. Already, other Aziza tribes have been attacked by his foul horde. That is why we must fight! We must band together if we are to defeat this threat, for he means to kill or imprison all of our kind in his search for the one of which the prophecy speaks."

Our kind, Asha thought. *I am one of them, too. An Aziza.*

"You are the one we have been waiting for," Pulligan said.

Asha almost laughed. "Why? There's nothing I can do. I have no power."

But immediately, she thought of the burning branch and killing one of the shadow men who had attacked her camp.

Pulligan smiled his awkward smile. "There is much for you to learn, Empress. For within you lies the power of a thousand suns."

Asha shook her head in disbelief. Everything she thought about herself was wrong. Why would Suna keep this from her?

A strange sensation rose up in Asha at that moment, one she was not familiar with. Her fists clenched, and she felt the blood thrumming in her ears.

Pulligan held up a hand. "Today has been a day of revelation. Let us take refreshment. The body needs sustenance."

In quick fashion, several Aziza men and women rose and disappeared down one of the tunnels. Asha watched as they faded to unseen points. She sat quietly, not knowing what to say. Obo peered around with a dazed expression. "Suna knew there was something special about you," he whispered. "Now we know what it is." He shook his head as if trying to make sense of it all.

Asha looked at her friend. "I don't know what is to come, Obo, but I'm glad you're here with me."

He smiled, and for a moment, she saw the old carefree Obo, the one who used to lift her over his head with one arm. She missed those days.

Her head was swimming with questions. Her parents might still be alive. They were taken, but there was no proof that the Shrike had killed them. She could hope. That's all she had. Hope.

Asha's thoughts were interrupted as the group of Aziza returned with refreshments.

They placed wooden bowls of grain, figs, and red berries before the assembled guests. Asha ate the food tentatively but found that her hunger was satiated. Sprix took to it immediately. Obo looked out of place among the diminutive Aziza people. He picked through the meager offerings. "No meat?" he asked, as politely as he could.

"This is food from the Mother Tree," Pulligan replied. "Our kind does not eat the flesh of animals. Our sustenance nourishes the body *and* mind. Partake and you shall see."

Obo poked his huge fingers around in the bowls in front of him, grabbing a small handful of each morsel. He chewed slowly, nodding. "Not bad," he muttered.

Asha tried some of the red berries and savored the taste. They were sweet and filled her with a warm glow. *This place is doing something to us,* Asha thought. *Something unusual.* She mustered up her courage and turned toward Pulligan. "The tree. I saw things when I touched it. What does it all mean?"

Pulligan's heavy-lidded eyes blinked slowly. "What you saw was meant for you only, Empress. No one else can understand its message. The Mother Tree knows all. The past, the future."

Asha remembered the face in her vision—a man with a bird mask who called her name.

Asha. It is time. We will meet soon.

The Shrike, she thought with dread. *My brother.*

I will defeat him. And find out what happened to my parents. No matter what it takes.

EIGHTEEN

THE SHINING SPEAR

AFTER THEIR MEAL, ASHA SAT quietly with her companions. All the revelations had taken a mental toll, and she felt as if she could fall asleep right there on the woven mats.

Never in a million years could she have imagined herself in such a situation. She thought of her old life of traveling from village to village, seeking plants in the forest for Suna, and sitting around a glowing fire listening to the griots as they spun their fantastical tales. She thought of Kowelo, and how he had tried to teach her to juggle. She would get so angry and frustrated. But she missed those lessons, and even his teasing. Now here she was, an empress, whatever that meant. She shook her head at the strangeness of it all.

She closed her eyes again for a brief moment, only to open them as footsteps sounded ahead of her. Two Aziza women were approaching, their faces set and determined. They bowed and then, without warning, took hold of Asha's arms on either side. Asha gasped and struggled. Obo and Rima were up in an instant.

"Do not fear, Empress," Pulligan said, holding up a hand. "They are here to help."

Asha let out a resigned breath. Even though she didn't know Pulligan at all, she was sure he wasn't an enemy or trickster. He wouldn't harm her, and whatever these women were going to do had his approval. She glanced at Rima and Obo and shrugged. "Okay," she relented.

The Aziza women led her away and down another maze of tunnels. Asha was too apprehensive to look at them, and instead focused on everything around her: the cool, damp air, the smell of smoke, and her footsteps on the smooth dirt path they walked upon. Eventually, the two women let go of her arms, for which she was grateful. Their grips were a little too strong.

She was led to a room with earthen walls and a

canvas-like cloth for a roof. Sheets of red and green fabric served as doors. Four candles upon a table illuminated the space. Several objects were placed on the table: a comb, brushes, and a few other small items.

What are those for? Asha thought.

A small Aziza child entered, carrying a large bowl of steaming hot water. He couldn't have been more than ten years old, but Asha could already see the timelessness in his eyes, as if he was wise beyond his years. He set the bowl on the table and left without saying a word.

To Asha's shock and embarrassment, the women tugged away her clothes and began scrubbing her from head to toe with stiff brushes. Again, Asha made to protest, but gave up quickly. She truly studied them for the first time and saw that their faces were old and weathered, dark eyes glittering in silence. Asha felt as if she were being rubbed raw. She tried to protest but was met more than once with a firm reprimand. "It is for you, Empress."

Asha didn't understand. It was as if they were preparing her for some sort of ceremony. As they continued to fuss over her, she thought about all she had just learned. She had a brother. "Adisa," she whispered. *What was he like before he became corrupted?* He was made fun of for looking different. *Do I look different?* These thoughts swirled in her head as the two women spun her around and continued their work. She thought of Rima, Obo, and Sprix and wondered what they were doing.

Asha felt odd and embarrassed that they were paying so much attention to her, and she didn't even know who they were. "What are your names?" she managed to ask.

The woman who was cleaning her fingernails with a fine slender twig said, "I am called Maet, Empress."

Empress . . . again.

"And I am called Rha, Empress," said the other, combing the knots out of her hair. Asha was reminded of Suna and she smiled.

"Maet and Rha," she said quietly. "Lovely names." But the two women went on as if they hadnt heard her.

After she was thoroughly scrubbed, they dressed her in a gown of brown and green, braided with soft strips of what seemed to be tree bark, held together by twigs and branches bound with tough vine. Oddly enough, it wasn't uncomfortable, and she found that she could move easily within it.

Maet tied a vine bracelet around one of Asha's ankles. Rha walked to the table and brought forth an intricately carved wooden box and withdrew a circlet of baobab leaves and placed it upon Asha's head. The two stepped away from her and studied her intently, as if she were a sculpture they had been working on.

"Now you are ready, Empress," Maet said reverently.

For what? Asha wondered.

She had no idea what she looked like in this new garb. There were no mirrors of any sort in the room— or anywhere else, she realized. They parted the red and green cloth and led Asha back the way they had come. To her utter surprise, men and women flanked the tunnels on either side, and as she passed them, they threw black flowers from the Mother Tree in her path.

They all think I'm some kind of queen, Asha realized. *An empress. I can't be their queen. I can't . . .*

After she had passed them, they joined in behind her, marching along in a straight line. The light from the torches they carried flickered on the walls.

The sound of music interrupted her thoughts, and it was unlike any she had heard before. It was percussive at its heart, filled with flutes, bells, and the soft beat of a drum; melancholy but also uplifting in an odd way.

As they made their way forward, the music became louder, until at last she saw a small band of Aziza in a circle playing curious instruments. But that was not the strangest thing. In the great cavern, hundreds of Aziza were gathered around the Mother Tree, as still as stones, as far as her eyes could see. Her friends were there as well, standing apart from the others. As she approached, she looked to Sprix, who actually clapped his hands together in glee. Obo and Rima looked on with pride and wonder.

Asha peered out at the faces of the Aziza. Hundreds of dark eyes looked back at her. Maet and Rha stopped in front of Pulligan, who stood before the Mother Tree and regarded Asha steadily. "Now you are ready," he said, as he laid a hand on Asha's shoulder, slightly turning her toward the audience. Asha swallowed. Her legs felt as if they were about to go out from under her again. It took every fiber of her being not to turn and run.

Pulligan held up his arms. "Today, we honor and welcome our empress, Asha, she of whom the prophecy speaks."

He clapped his hands and a man came forth from the crowd. He carried something in his outstretched hands, palms up.

"It is said," Pulligan continued, as the man paused in front of him, "that when the day comes, our empress shall wield a great weapon, one that only she can bear."

He stared at her for a long moment. "And if she is not worthy, she will be struck down where she stands."

Asha swallowed hard. Pulligan's eyes shone with a fierce spark.

Struck down? By whom, or what?

The man bowed his head in front of Asha and thrust out his arms, offering the deadly prize. Asha saw that it was a spear, carved from a rich, black wood. Knots and whorls were clearly visible along its length, and at the tip, a green gem shone in the dark.

"Empress," Pulligan said, "take this weapon into your hands. May the blessing of the Royal Lioness guide you."

Asha exhaled. She looked to her friends. Obo smiled and nodded. Sprix looked on in anticipation. Rima's eyes were unreadable.

Asha reached out. *Please don't strike me down. Please don't strike me down . . .*

She grasped the spear.

She waited for the unimaginable to happen—the ground beneath her feet opening up and swallowing her, a bolt of lightning crashing down to burn her to cinders—but nothing came. Instead, the wood was cool to the touch, and Asha felt a tingle run up her arm and down her spine. She grasped the spear with both hands and raised it, and the gem at its point flashed from green to cold white, illuminating the dim cave into daylight. Asha wanted to shield her eyes, but did not.

"The spear is called Frost," Pulligan said, "and has been with us since time began. You, Asha, are its bearer." He held up his hands. "Behold our empress, Asha! She Who Brings Light!"

Asha held the shining spear above her head as the Aziza raised their voices in celebration.

NINETEEN

KEEPER OF SONGS

AFTER THE CEREMONY, Maet and Rha led Asha and her friends to a quiet room away from the Mother Tree. It was a small space with a dirt floor covered by soft woven mats. A few chairs and tables were placed about and, like elsewhere in the kingdom, torches affixed to the wall provided light. The furniture was carved from smooth, blond wood with intricate leaf patterns etched into the grain. Everything here was made from nature, Asha realized, including the Aziza's clothing. She looked down at her own clothes and felt a little out of place among her more humbly dressed companions.

Asha sat in one of the chairs with the spear, Frost, across her knees. She felt strange having such a powerful weapon meant only for her.

Obo rose from the ground where he sat and drew close to Asha. The chairs were just too small for his large frame. "It is a beautiful spear," he said, admiring it. "May I, Empress?"

Asha closed her eyes in irritation. She handed him the spear.

Obo took it carefully, as if afraid it would burst into flame. She supposed that others could touch it but not actually use it in battle. He hefted it in his hands, ran his fingers along the wood. "Perfectly balanced," he said. "We'll have to do some training, yeah?"

Asha was stunned. She didn't know how to use a weapon. What was she supposed to do with it, roast a rabbit? "Yes," she managed to say. "I suppose so."

Obo stared at her. In awe, it seemed to Asha.

"I just never could have imagined it," Asha continued after a moment. "Me? Some kind of queen? It doesn't make sense."

"The gods work in mysterious ways, Empress," Rima said.

Asha threw up her hands. "Okay! Enough! All of you! My name is Asha!"

"Yes, Emp—" Obo began, but Asha shot him a withering look that sent him into silence. Sprix laughed at the whole spectacle.

"I don't want to be an empress," Asha pouted.

"It is your destiny," Rima replied.

"I just want to know what happened to my parents. My . . . brother . . . Adisa. I need to find him, ask him why he did all this. Why didn't Suna tell me about my mother and father?"

Rima shook her head. "I think she didn't want to give you hope."

"Hope?"

"Yes. Hope that they could still be alive."

"They are alive," Asha said. "I know it."

"Let that be your destiny, then," Rima encouraged her. "Let that drive you forward."

Asha didn't reply. But she took Rima's advice to heart.

Asha's perception of time had been lost since she'd entered the Underground Kingdom. She remembered that they had arrived during the night, but she couldn't recall if it was the night before this one or if two nights had passed. Her head still swirled with questions.

The Shrike. My brother.

She lay on her back, a soft mat beneath her. Her companions had been led to their own quarters, not far from hers. Asha's place of rest was an opening carved into the cave wall, which led to a long tunnel where she had her own private space. An Aziza warrior stood outside of it, keeping guard, which made Asha self-conscious. "Empress," she whispered, a note of disdain in her voice.

Her bed was braided branches overlaid with soft woven mats of some type of grass. She was comfortable, but it did feel a little damp. Small lights twinkled above her, some sort of mineral or gem embedded in the cave roof, she guessed. The air was cool, but not cold enough for her to lie under blankets, which she had tossed to the cave floor.

Asha's ears perked up at the sound of singing.

It was a woman's voice, high and bright. The song was trance-like, and for a moment Asha thought she might cry from the sheer beauty of it. Instead, she decided to find its source.

She sat up and grabbed her spear. Not that she thought she would need it; she just wanted to keep it close. It was hers, through destiny.

Her guard gave her a surprised look when he saw her, but Asha only smiled and said, "I will be back. I only need to stretch my legs."

The man nodded once and then became as still as stone. Asha hoped that she wasn't going to get him in trouble.

Darkness closed in around her as she walked out of the cave and into the larger cavern. She tensed as Frost's tip flared with a cold, bright light, giving her a path. Dotted here and there, small fires burned with Aziza huddled around them. It seemed to Asha that life in the cave did have a system of sorts. Just like her dwelling, she saw several carved or naturally made openings that led into larger living quarters. But outside those homes, if they could be called that, the open caverns seemed more communal, where families and neighbors came together.

As Asha walked, footsteps sounded behind her. She turned, her vision sharp from Frost's light. It was her guard, far enough away to not intrude, but close enough to keep watch. And here she thought he was going to remain at his post.

Asha smiled, but she hoped the guard didn't see. She

didn't want to be treated any differently than anyone else. But she knew that wasn't possible. She was an empress, She Who Brings Light.

She continued on and came to a place where the reddish rock gave way to white limestone. Several drawings were revealed here. One of them took up a long, vertical strip, and showed what appeared to be a battle. Other drawings were of an imaginative nature and seemed to be for worship. The Royal Lioness with bared teeth; the Sea Eagle, soaring over wavy lines symbolizing water.

Asha turned away as the woman's voice rose on the air, first high, then low. She followed it as the keening grew louder. She was close now. Ahead of her, a small fire flickered, flames dancing in the dark. A woman sat cross-legged before it. She looked up as Asha approached.

"Empress." The woman dipped her head.

"I do not mean to disturb you," Asha said. "I heard your singing. It's beautiful."

"It is a song of battle. I am Pande-Kura, Keeper of Songs. Sit with me, child."

Asha sat down and placed Frost on the ground beside her, and the shining gem at its tip immediately dimmed. The woman before Asha was old. Her face was a continent of lines and wrinkles. Long gray hair tied in two braids fell to her shoulders. Her eyes were like every other Aziza's, large and almond-shaped, except they were an uncanny green instead of brown. Asha swallowed. "Keeper of Songs. What songs?"

"All songs. All of the Aziza songs, since the beginning."

Pande-Kura wore a flat red stone around her neck that caught the flames of the fire and sparkled. "The beginning?" Asha ventured.

"Songs have power, child. If we were to lose them, we would lose ourselves, no?"

"I suppose so," Asha said, trying to work it out in her head.

"We sing to the gods and ancestors for protection and strength. For battle. For love. For life. There are not many Song Keepers left. I must continue the songs."

Asha nodded. "And who will keep them going when you—" She stopped short, realizing her question might have been rude.

Pande-Kura's green eyes flickered. "There are many who would seek to take up the songs when I pass from this world. But first, the gods must find them worthy. It is hard work, and not everyone who sings becomes Keeper."

Asha nodded. The fire was burning low, yellow

flames casting shadows onto the old woman's face. "And the song you were singing, you said it was a song for battle?"

Pande-Kura took a branch from the ground beside her and poked the fire. A green flame went up, whooshing into the air. "Yes, child. Battle is drawing near. I can feel it."

Asha swallowed and looked into her lap. "They expect me to do something great. To lead. I don't even know how to fight."

She felt like a small child, complaining about something trivial. But this wasn't trivial. Asha sensed it was a matter of life and death.

"You will find your bravery," Pande-Kura said.

The old woman rested her open palms on her knees and closed her eyes. She began to sing again, a hypnotic tapestry of sound and emotion, which immediately put Asha at ease. She could have sworn she saw flames rising from Pande-Kura's weathered hands, as if she were holding two orbs. Sparks seemed to dance in front of her like tiny yellow ghosts.

It can't be, Asha thought. *I'm seeing things.*

But as she continued to watch, her head light on her shoulders, the balls of flame went from yellow to red and then to green, spinning and spinning the whole while.

Pande-Kura sang, and Asha felt every emotion flood her heart—from joy to longing to sadness. Then, with one final note that rose into the air and floated to the top of the cave, the song came to an end. The old woman opened her eyes. "Now you are ready, Empress."

"Ready? For what?"

"War."

Asha stiffened.

Pande-Kura's eyes seemed to pierce Asha's soul. "Yes, child. War. Do not fear. This song is like armor. It will protect you. But even armor can be pierced by the dark. Trust yourself, and the spear you carry. Let your heart guide you."

From the corner of Asha's vision, Frost gleamed with a cold, white light.

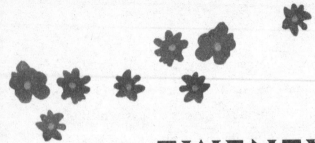

TWENTY

TWO WARRIORS

"AGAIN," OBO DEMANDED, circling Asha. "One. Two. Three. *Strike!*"

Asha planted her feet and swung the spear once more. She felt the air ripple as she brought it down, but Obo stepped aside as easily as a cat, which seemed strange for a man his size.

Asha fumed. She just wasn't very good at fighting. "Maybe my strength lies elsewhere," she said, winded.

"It will come," Obo encouraged her. "You just need more practice."

Asha winced, remembering Kowelo and his juggling

lessons. "I have this weapon that is supposed to be so important and I can barely wield it."

In answer, Obo swung his staff in an attempt to hit Asha's left side. Instinctively, she raised Frost and blocked the blow.

"You did it!" Obo cried out.

Sprix, sitting nearby with Rima, clapped furiously.

Frost still vibrated in Asha's hands. She could almost *hear* it. A hum that rang in her ears.

"Don't think of it as a weapon," Obo said, circling her like a giant bear. "Think of it as a part of you."

Asha breathed in rhythm with her heartbeat as she moved around Obo. *Pulligan says I have power. I need to find it. Use it.*

She spun quickly to her right and whirled the staff above her head before going low, trying to take Obo's feet out from under him.

Strike! she shouted in her head.

Obo went down like a felled tree.

"Oof," he grunted.

"Are you okay?" Asha asked, offering a hand.

Obo pulled himself up on his own. He let out a breath. "That was very good, Emp—Asha." He bent down a little and looked her in the eye. "Now, if you can do that a hundred more times, you'll be on your way to becoming a true fighter."

Asha sighed.

Asha and Obo spent an hour training every day. After several sessions, she was finally becoming familiar with the weight and feel of the spear. The more she used it, the more it became a part of her, as Obo had said. It fit her grip by some strange magic, and sometimes felt light as a feather. It was as if the spear sensed when it was being used for deadly force and when it was not. Whatever magic it held, Asha was glad she was the one to possess it.

When she wasn't training with Obo or sharing meals with her friends, she often set out on her own to explore the Underground Kingdom. She felt she had to sneak away to do this, as she was sure Pulligan would send some sort of royal guard along with her had he known, even though there was nothing here to fear.

One day, she came upon two young women, the first she had seen that were of an age with her. They were locked in a battle of sorts, one with a short spear and the other armed with only a long length of rope with a loop at the end.

Asha stood a few feet away and watched them spar. The girl with the spear certainly seemed to have an advantage over the other, but Asha was surprised when rope girl flicked her wrist, looped the end of her rope around her opponent's weapon, and yanked hard. The other girl flew forward, dropping her spear as she did so.

"Nice attack, Sabra, but I think you got lucky."

The girl called Sabra threw her head back and laughed, a high, tinkling sound that Asha thought pleasant. Only then did they see her watching from a few paces back. Their demeanor immediately changed.

"Empress," they both said, bowing their heads.

Asha breathed through her nose. "Please," she said. "It's Asha."

The three girls sat in a circle in a small hollow space surrounded by black rocks. Sabra's sparring partner was named Kalasha. Asha loved the Aziza names. She didn't know their meanings yet, but she was fascinated by them.

Sabra was the same height as Asha, with black hair tied up on her head with two gold sticks. Her eyes were like Pande-Kura's, green, while Kalasha's were deep brown. Silvery, straight hair framed Kalasha's oval face.

Asha told them about Suna and everything that had happened since she had set out with Obo.

"I will stand by your side," Sabra said.

"As will I," added Kalasha.

"Thank you," Asha replied, not quite knowing if that was the right response. But the two girls seemed to accept it. Sabra opened a pouch and took out some dried papaya, which they all shared.

"How many battles have you seen?" Kalasha asked.

Asha almost gagged on her fruit. "None, really. Well, one. When our camp was attacked and Suna . . ."

Kalasha dipped her head in respect. She touched her forehead and then her heart. "I am sorry, Empress. I forgot that you have suffered a great loss."

"It is fine, Kalasha."

"We have not been in battle, either," Sabra said. "But we will gladly follow you to the ends of Alkebulan to defeat the Shrike. He has killed our kind. That cannot go unchallenged."

Kalasha nodded in fierce agreement.

Asha was honored that these two young Aziza warriors would defend her. Something inside her shifted at that moment. She realized that she was someone the Aziza looked to for strength. Someone they would protect and follow. She had to be strong for them, no matter what. *I promise*, she told herself. *I promise not to let you all down.*

"Now," Sabra said. "Let's see what you can do with that spear, Empress."

Asha spent the next few hours with Sabra and Kalasha. They showed her many things, including how to stand when delivering a blow, and how to use your fingers, elbows, and knees as weapons. By the time they were done, Asha was sweating and her muscles ached.

"You will be a great fighter," Sabra said.

Asha wasn't so sure.

"When the time comes," Kalasha added, "you will be ready."

"That's just it," Asha said, mopping her brow with her hand. "I don't know if I *want* the time to come. I want to find out what happened to my mother and father, but . . . I'm afraid of what I will learn."

"Knowing your fear will help you defeat it," Sabra said.

"I want to avenge Suna and the others," Asha said. "They were my family. But the Shrike . . . he is my brother.

I do not want to kill him."

It was true, Asha knew. Even if he was an evil sorcerer, he was her blood. Still, he had to be stopped and punished. How?

For a moment, no one spoke and the space around them was quiet, but for the sound of dripping water in the distance.

"You will know, Empress," Kalasha said. "Your heart will decide for you."

Asha exhaled a worried, frustrated breath. She hoped that when the day came, Kalasha's words would ring true.

TWENTY-ONE

TO ARMS

ASHA SAT WITH HER FRIENDS in one of the common areas of the cave. Several stalactites, their points sharp and heavy, hung from the roof above them. Sprix was worried they might fall, but one of the Aziza reassured him that magic held them in place. Sprix stared up in fascination. For a moment, Asha believed it, until the Aziza man looked at her and winked.

As a low fire burned before them, Asha and her companions shared dried fruit and nuts. Her arms and legs were still sore from her training with Kalasha and Sabra. She was practicing every day, but to what end? She wasn't sure what the next step was. How could she lead the Aziza people? She wasn't ready yet, and she didn't know when she would be. Was Pulligan waiting for her to rally the troops and call them to battle? How would they even get to the Burned Lands, the Shrike's—her brother's—domain?

"Where does the water come from?" Sprix asked, breaking Asha's thoughts.

"Huh?" Asha replied.

"The water we drink," he continued. "Where does it come from?"

"That's a good question, Sprix," Asha said. She looked at Obo, who raised his shoulders in doubt.

"Come," Rima said. "I will show you."

Rima led the way and they followed.

"I came upon it the other day when I was exploring," Rima called back.

There were all kinds of paths in the cave, some narrow and some broad. They went in all directions. Asha wondered how the Aziza avoided getting lost. Then again, if she had spent all of her life below ground, she'd probably know her way around, too.

They passed several Aziza, some weaving baskets while others used small, fine tools to create decorative objects from wood or stone. They sang as they worked, and Asha noticed that all the songs were melancholy. There was a sadness to these people, but also strength. When they saw her, they would dip their heads for a moment, a gesture of respect. Asha didn't really like it, but there was nothing she could do to prevent it.

"Here we are," Rima said, bringing them to a stop.

They were standing before a crack in the cave wall. It was only a few feet across. Asha peered at it with a skeptical eye.

"In there?" Obo asked, glancing at the opening doubt-fully.

"I thought you weren't afraid of anything," Rima pressed him.

Obo, never one to back down from a challenge, puffed out his chest. "I'm not," he said.

Asha swallowed. It looked as if the opening was barely big enough for Obo's broad shoulders.

"I'm not scared, either," Sprix put in, and slipped into the crevice.

Rima followed him. Asha stared at Obo, who let out a breath, as if he were trying to lose a few pounds just by exhaling.

"You don't have to go," Asha said.

It was meant as reassurance, but Obo took it as an insult. He huffed, bowed his head, and slipped in behind Rima, squeezing his way in.

"Here goes," said Asha, and she slid through.

The space was tight and damp. Water dripped onto Asha's head. She could already hear Obo's and Rima's voices ahead of her, echoing. A minute later, she stepped out into a large cavern.

"By the Five," she exclaimed.

Ahead of them, a shimmering waterfall cascaded down into a large pool, surrounded by massive gray stones. The air was cool here, and green lichen clung to the wall like a tapestry. Asha took a deep breath, filling her lungs. Sprix dashed off to the cave pool and went in up to his knees. He cupped his hands and drank. "It's so good!" he shouted, his voice echoing.

Asha joined Sprix and drank as well. The water was fresh and invigorating, and seemed to focus her thoughts. They basked in the moment, relaxing in the cool air. After a time, Obo drew near to Asha. "What have you heard?" he asked. "From Pulligan. What does he plan to do?"

"I don't know," Asha replied. "I don't know what to say to him. I still feel like all of this isn't real, I guess."

It was true, Asha knew that for certain. She could

have sought Pulligan out herself, asked him what her role was supposed to be. But she also felt that if she was meant to be doing something he would let her know. She found the whole idea of her being a leader hard to accept.

"Am I supposed to gather everyone and march to the Burned Lands?" Asha asked. "He's their leader."

"Maybe he waits for you to command him," Obo ventured.

Their conversation was interrupted by the sound of approaching voices. Asha turned toward the entrance. Three Aziza warriors, one man and two women, were gathered there, armed with spears.

"Empress," one of the women said. "You are needed. Pulligan seeks you."

Asha looked to Obo and gulped.

The three warriors led them back through the narrow crevice. *What is happening?* Asha thought, as she followed the Aziza. They were silent as they marched, their backs stiff and straight. Asha heard the murmur of voices as they walked. Finally, in the distance, she saw the Mother Tree. And people were gathered around it.

As they drew closer, Asha saw that several of them were holding torches. Pulligan stood at the front. As always, he was dressed in hues of green and brown. A breastplate that looked like it was made of wood covered his chest. His face was grim. Asha felt her stomach tighten. There was some news to be had and she was sure it wasn't good. She just knew.

"Empress," Pulligan said. "I have a troubling report. Spies have been discovered on our borders. Our friends the Rowan Circle captured some of them, but not before a few escaped. They will no doubt hurry back and tell the Shrike our location."

"What does this mean?" Obo asked. "For us, and . . . the empress?"

"It means the time to strike is now," Pulligan said.

A tremor ran through Asha's body. So soon? How could it be? She wasn't ready! She thought she'd have many more days to plan and prepare.

"What do we do?" she asked.

Pulligan's gaze drifted over her, and then to Obo, Rima, and Sprix. "We take the fight to them. Come. Follow me."

It's happening, Asha thought, her stomach knotted with fear. *War is coming*. Pulligan led them deeper into the tunnels. Asha held Frost in a sweating fist. Sprix followed as quietly as a fox behind them.

"Do not fear," Rima said. "We are with you, Asha."

"We stand together," Obo added. Asha didn't answer, distracted by the sound of drums that rose on the air. She felt each beat in her heart, as heavy as hammer strokes.

Boom. Boom. Boom.

Pulligan led them around a corner and Asha gasped.

In another enormous cavern, hundreds of men and women with spears, shields, and short swords stood at attention. Behind them were rows of archers with small bows and full quivers across their backs. All their faces were hard and unsmiling.

Pulligan stood before them, then walked along their ranks, nodding in approval. "It has been many a year since the Aziza tribes have gathered for war. We have remained hidden, causing harm to none, but today, that ends. Today, we fight together!"

The Aziza warriors remained silent, as still as statues.

"The Shrike is seeking our empress," Pulligan went on, "she who is foretold in prophecy. She carries the great spear Frost, which will lead us to battle. Today, we march against the Shrike!"

A roar went up, and spears clashed against shields. Asha almost raised her hands to her ears because it was so loud, but quickly realized that certainly wouldn't look right.

RONALD L. SMITH

"Chestnut Clan!" Pulligan shouted. "Ivy Grove! Moringa Spears! We fight together!"

Asha felt the ground rumble with the stamping of many feet. She looked out at the different clans. Some had markings on their faces—lines, spirals, and other shapes. They were all diminutive in stature, but some had markings on their faces—lines, spirals, and other shapes. Another thing they all shared was the fierceness of their eyes.

Pulligan held up a hand and the crowd fell quiet. "We do this today in honor of our empress. She has come to throw down our enemy. Behold! She Who Brings Light!"

Another cry went up, followed by hundreds more. "Asha! Asha! Asha!"

Asha swallowed hard and tried to look as brave as possible.

After the celebratory chants, the warriors grew quiet again, and Pulligan's gaze fell on Asha. *He wants me to say something. By the Five.*

She scanned the assembled masses before her. The great cavern was dark, but the torches provided enough light for her to see Sabra and Kalasha standing proudly in the first row.

Pulligan turned to Asha and stretched out his arm,

beckoning. Asha gulped.

She took a step forward, Frost gripped tightly in her hand. *Here goes,* she thought, not really knowing what she was going to say. She exhaled, still taking in the scene before her, the dancing lights and the countless warriors. "Aziza people," she began, hoping her voice was strong enough. "You have welcomed me and my companions into your kingdom and treated us with respect." She caught Obo's nod and his smile urged her on.

"The Shrike must be stopped. He has killed many of you, and . . . someone dear to me." She sniffed. "And now, his time has come."

"Yes!" shouted a warrior.

"He must be thrown down!" Asha said, gaining confidence.

"We are with you, Empress!"

Asha felt it now, pride and vengeance swelling up inside her.

"He must be defeated!"

In the distance, Pande-Kura's melancholy battle song floated out over the crowd.

"We will strike hard and true!"

Asha continued to speak, and the stamping of feet and the lilting voice became a symphony.

"We will give no mercy!"

She held up her spear and, as if her will commanded it, the gem at its point flared with white light.

"Aziza!" she cried, and the voices of hundreds of warriors joined her. "We! Are! Aziza!"

TWENTY-TWO

THE TOWER

ASHA'S BATTLE CRY IGNITED A flame within her belly. As she looked out over the gathered Aziza tribes, she felt a sense of pride and purpose she had never experienced before. This was her destiny. What she was meant to do.

Pulligan approached her and gave a slight nod. "I must speak with the clan leaders. We must leave before daybreak."

Asha didn't know what to say. "We will be ready," she finally said.

Rima, Obo, and Sprix gathered by her side as several

warriors followed Pulligan down one of the numerous tunnels.

Obo stood before Asha and studied her for a moment.

"What is it?" Asha asked.

Obo knelt on one knee and held his staff lengthwise as if in offering. "I will follow you, Empress."

He bowed his head.

Rima brandished her spear and knelt also. "I swear allegiance to Asha. She Who Brings Light. You have my spear."

Asha choked back tears. She sniffed and rubbed her eyes.

Sprix, the boy with so many mysteries, bowed his head and followed suit. "I am with you . . . Empress. You saved my life. And I, um, will defend yours as best I can."

Now Asha was overcome. "Oh, get up all of you!" she burst out, laughing and crying at the same time. "I am so proud of you. I couldn't ask for better friends."

They had little time to bask in the moment. Pulligan soon returned and urged them to make final preparations. Asha and the others went about gathering food, weapons, and other supplies for the journey. Sabra fitted her with a tough vine belt that held a sheath and a short, sharp dagger. She was also given thick wooden armor that protected her torso.

They departed under the cover of night. Sabra and Kalasha took it upon themselves to become Asha's personal guards and would not leave her side. She walked with Pulligan, together with Rima, Obo, and Sprix. Fifteen or twenty warriors followed behind and in front, providing a solid battalion. Asha was marching to war. *War.*

After two days of traveling, Asha, Sabra, and Kalasha sat together in a circle while the rest of the camp prepared for the evening meal. "Empress," Sabra began, even though Asha had repeatedly told them both to call her Asha. "Tell us of your Suna. What was she like?"

Asha felt a pang of sadness at the mention of her name. She shifted on the ground. "She was like a mother to me. Sometimes she would make me angry. But other times she would know just what to say to make me feel wanted and loved."

Sabra and Kalasha peered at Asha as the fire crackled.

"I wish I could be more like her."

Asha stopped then, not knowing what else to say, and stared into the flames.

"You will find your courage," Sabra said.

"They will sing songs of you in years to come," Kalasha added.

Asha laughed then, a little too loudly.

"I have seen it," Kalasha said.

Asha raised an eyebrow.

"In my dreams, you are a bright, shining light, which will strike down our enemy."

Asha tensed. She was troubled by everyone's belief in her—Pulligan and all her friends. What if she couldn't defeat the Shrike? What if they were all marching to their deaths?

"She is a seer," Sabra explained, bringing Asha back to the moment.

"I'm still learning the path," Kalasha put in. "It takes many years to reach true foresight and wisdom."

Asha was reminded of her tea reading and wondered if she'd ever do it again. "I hope your dreams are true, Kalasha, and that I don't let you down."

I hope I don't, Asha thought. *I hope.*

For three more nights they made their way through forests and slept out in the open, as Aziza warriors took turns standing watch. The meals were few and the hours of travel long. Asha had hoped some kind of Aziza magic could sweep them away to the Burned Lands, but nothing of the sort was offered. They had been walking for days, and Asha felt as if she could go no farther. Her feet were sore and her muscles ached.

"Not too far now, Empress," Pulligan encouraged her. But his words were little comfort. She was fatigued, urged on only by the will of her companions.

Small cookfires dotted the area where they had made camp. A ring of marula trees formed a barrier of sorts, a wide circle that enclosed them so they would not be visible to their enemies. Asha sat with her friends, staring into the flames of their fire. The smell of roasting meat drifted over them. Pulligan sat nearby, sharpening a short blade on a flat stone. "Tell me of your people, child," he said without taking his eyes off his work.

Asha and Sprix glanced at one another, not sure who Pulligan was addressing. Finally, Sprix looked left, then right, and then pointed to himself. "Me?"

Pulligan nodded. "Yes . . . *Sprix*." He pronounced his name with difficulty, as if the combination of letters was not easy for his tongue to decipher.

Sprix eyed Asha and then looked back to Pulligan. "I don't remember," he said. "My . . . father, Finn, said I was left by the faeries, and they took his real son."

Pulligan cocked his head. "Faeries," he said slowly. "I have heard of your kind. They are called the Seelie Court, and live way beyond this world."

Sprix's eyes lit up. "Seelie Court?"

"Yes. Your race is similar to ours, but we do not have this power to"—he waved his free hand in the air—"transform ourselves."

Sprix turned a shade of red, as if Pulligan knowing this about him was an invasion of his privacy.

"How did you know?" Asha asked. "That Sprix can change?"

"The Aziza can sense these things, Empress. Things that are part of an older world. Things that sometimes remain hidden."

Asha wondered if she had this ability as well. She had known that Sprix was different when they'd first met, but she hadn't known exactly how.

"The Seelie Court is . . . benevolent," Pulligan continued. "But the Unseelie Court—" He drew a finger across his throat.

"They . . . kill people?" Sprix asked.

"They have no love for humankind," Pulligan said, "and they take up space in the dark places of the world.

Your people, the Seelie, are more kind to humans, and they are often seen in the company of human kings and queens."

Sprix stared, wide-eyed. "I don't know why I was put with Finn, the terrible man who raised me. There was a lady, too, who lived with him. His wife. She . . . she ran away. He took it out on me."

Pulligan nodded. "It wasn't any fault of yours, child. Maybe this man wronged the faeries, and they took his son as revenge. Or perhaps, by placing you in a human home, your kind thought you could have a better life. It is not for me to know." He went back to sharpening his knife.

Sprix lowered his head. Asha reached out and touched his hand. "You have a family now, Sprix. We won't abandon you."

Sprix squeezed her hand in return.

A moment of silence passed where the only sound in the forest was the sharpening of Pulligan's blade. Asha had been wanting to learn more about the Aziza, and it seemed like a good time to ask.

"Could you tell me about the different Aziza tribes?" Asha finally asked him.

Pulligan tested his blade on a piece of wood. "When we roamed Alkebulan freely, we were often at war with one another. The Rowan Circle was aligned with us, the Baobab Circle. But the Chestnut Clan usually remained with the Ivy Grove and the Moringa Spears. We battled so long I do not even remember the reasons. Food and water. The bounty of the land. But we came to realize we had to band together and remain hidden if we were to survive. Now we have strength in numbers."

Asha marveled at the history she was now a part of.

Pulligan looked up from his work. "Now we stand together, with you leading us."

Asha smiled weakly.

They slept for only snatches at a time as they trudged on, over small hills and dry ravines. There were caves and hidden places in the forest where they rested during the day, and they moved stealthily at night. One time, Asha saw Pulligan and some of the other Aziza leaders huddle together, and when they parted, she could have sworn a veil seemed to settle over the camp, like a blanket of stars. Maybe this was the Aziza magic she'd been hoping to see, protecting them somehow.

Finally, after many nights of travel, they made their way through a wood of stunted trees and came into an open plain. After being under the heavy canopy of leaves and branches for so long the sunlight blazed in Asha's vision. The forest was at their back now, and ahead of them was only dry earth. It seemed to go on as far as Asha's eyes could see. But the expansive, barren ground was not what drew Asha's attention. In the distance, a tower of black rock rose into the air as if it could pierce the very heavens.

There were no signs of life anywhere. Except for one. Black birds—shrikes—perched at the very top of the tower, as if standing watch.

Pulligan took in the scene before them. Asha stood to his left with Sabra and Kalasha, while Obo, Sprix, and Rima were on his right.

"The Shrike's Nest," Rima declared.

Asha looked upon the tower with dread. *My mother and father are in there. I hope.*

"What do we do now?" Sprix asked.

As if in answer, the shrikes sent up a raucous alarm.

"That's it," Obo said. "They know we're here."

The Aziza warriors formed lines behind Pulligan, holding their weapons at the ready. Asha wondered what she should do. She gripped Frost a little more tightly. She still didn't really know how to fight. The few lessons she'd had with Obo, Sabra, and Kalasha seemed to flee from her memory. But she remembered her battle call to the warriors before they'd departed the kingdom. *He must be thrown down! He must be defeated!*

A deafening horn blast shattered Asha's thoughts.

She felt as if her very bones would crack from the sound.

Again it blared.

And again.

Asha looked in the direction of the sound. She narrowed her eyes, and her breath suddenly caught in her throat.

Massive iron doors at the base of the tower swung outward, and from it advanced a horde of creatures. Rank upon rank of figures poured forth, like ants from a mound. A cloud of dust rose from their heavy footfalls as they marched forward.

"Tokoloshe!" Pulligan hissed. "Many of them. Foul creatures of the dark!"

Tokoloshe, Asha thought with dread, even though she had never heard the word before.

Pulligan held out his arms. "Aziza!" he cried.

The Aziza warriors behind him snapped to attention. They formed a long, rectangular block, with archers in the back and spears in the front.

Asha turned to Sprix. "This is it. Are you ready?"

In answer, Sprix closed his eyes for a brief moment, and when he opened them again, they held a wild glow. "Ready, Empress," he said.

"Empress," Pulligan called. "Believe in yourself. Let Frost guide you. Do not fear! You are Aziza!"

Asha looked at Pulligan. His weathered face showed just the hint of a smile. "I won't," she replied. "I am ready."

Obo laid a heavy hand on her shoulder. "We have come a long way, Asha. We will avenge Suna. This I know. May the Royal Lioness guide you."

Asha swallowed and felt a stinging in her eyes. "I am glad you are with me, Obo."

She turned to face the Tokoloshe. She felt as if her spine were rattling from their advancing footfalls. They were closing in. *When is Pulligan going to give the order to charge?*

As if he had read her thoughts, Pulligan held up an arm. "Archers!" he called. "Nock!"

In one fluid motion, hundreds of Aziza warriors drew back their bows.

"Hold!" he shouted.

Asha waited for the final command, her heart beating faster than ever before.

And with a downward slash of his arm, Pulligan cried, "Loose!"

Asha heard the bowstrings creak as the deadly arrows whizzed above her head.

And then, with a bloodcurdling cry, the Shrike's horde closed in on them.

They fell upon the Aziza in a rush. Asha backed up and crouched in a defensive position, holding her spear lengthways with both hands. Her heart pounded in her chest. One of the creatures—a Tokoloshe with a dented sword—lunged at her, a hulking shape of claws, hair, and black teeth. Instinctively, she raised Frost, and, to her amazement, the spear blocked the blow. She gasped as the beast flew back and crashed to the ground with a thud.

Sprix. Asha snapped her head left, then right. *Where is he?* And then she saw him. A few feet away, he swiveled to dodge a sword thrust and dropped to his knees. Asha rushed in and slammed the butt of her spear into the Tokoloshe's chest. Sprix shook his head, as if in pain. But then Asha saw his form writhe and contort, his skin weaving into something unknown. In the blink of an eye, it was done, and it almost took Asha's breath away.

Sprix was a fox, a large one, with bristling red hair standing up on his back. For one brief moment he glanced at Asha, and then he dove at the Tokoloshe, lunging at their ankles, hamstringing them, and bringing them down in cries of pain.

"Amazing," Asha whispered, as she turned her attention back to the raging fight around them.

Sabra and Kalasha stayed close, defending her, knocking back the enemy with their weapons. Asha had never seen such amazing fighters before. They moved fluidly, gracefully, like deadly dancers armed to kill.

Obo's whip seemed alive as it lashed out, twining around necks or legs, and sending the foul creatures into a blind frenzy.

But with a sinking feeling, Asha heard a sound she knew—a droning buzz that grew in her ears. She looked up at the sky. The dragonflies and their ghastly riders were back, the ones they had fought while following the Golden Path. There were hundreds of them, buzzing and clacking.

Asha raised her spear again and swung, sending one, now two barreling away from her. They spun out of control and hit the dry ground, but then, just like before, the small beetle-like riders rose up and attacked. Asha swung Frost in a wide arc, sweeping them away. Sprix was there in an instant, clamping down with sharp teeth and whipping his head back and forth. Meanwhile, more of the Tokoloshe were advancing, as if they had singled her out as the prize their master wanted.

"Asha!" Rima cried, rushing to her aid. Her leaf-bladed spear twirled above her head, felling the enemy with deadly accuracy, knocking out Tokoloshe after Tokoloshe.

Over and over Asha gripped Frost and connected with the creatures, sending them down to the dusty plain of battle.

For a quick moment, Asha and Rima locked eyes in celebration of their combined effort, but the joy was short-lived. As Asha looked on in horror, even more ranks of the Shrike's horde advanced from the tower. They bore black banners emblazoned with a shrike's head, and as they marched forward, clashing their weapons against their shields, they cried out a single word, and it made Asha's hair stand up on end:

"*Shrike!*"

"*Shrike!*"

"*Shrike!*"

That's it, Asha thought. *Our luck is over.*

Then, right at that moment, the ground began to tremble. There was a moment of stillness as the fighting slowed; even the enemy stopped and looked for the source of the great drumming below their feet. All eyes turned to the east, and under the blazing sun, Asha smiled.

"Toru!" she cried. "It's Toru!"

With the deafening sound of thundering hoof beats, Toru, the Great Father of the Forest, charged down the plain with his army of Gazella, a storm of dust in their wake. He rode with his captains Ossia and Rasha on either side, and their eyes blazed with fire.

"For the empress!" Toru cried, as his herd joined the fray. A hundred antlers, like deadly sharp spears, drove the horde back, tossing and lifting them into the air.

"He told me we would meet again," Asha whispered.

"Yes!" Obo cheered, as Toru's army wielded glowing orbs of fire between their antlers that became missiles of flame, destroying everything in their path.

Asha felt renewed hope as the battle raged on, now led by the great gazelles of the forest. The Tokoloshe snarled and chattered gibberish as they fought. Chaos reigned, but the Gazella held back the hideous beasts.

Obo switched between his whip and his pine staff, a deadly combination that left no mercy. Asha rushed to his side and brought down two more of the dragonfly riders, her spear like a branch of fire in her hands.

A few steps away, one of Pulligan's warriors was

being overwhelmed, but she was fighting back fiercely. Asha turned from Obo and sent the enemy scurrying with savage thrusts and blows. She still couldn't quite believe she was knocking down the vile monsters. She was terrified, but Frost propelled her forward.

Then, just as quickly as it started, it was over. Bodies lay crumpled and broken all across the desolate plain. Asha tore her eyes away from the carnage and looked to the tower. *My parents*, she thought. *I have to go inside and look for them.*

But the battle was not done.

In the distance, a lone rider emerged from the tower's gate. Dust stirred under the horse's hooves, a great white steed with a mane of yellow.

It began to gallop, coming closer. "On your guard," Asha said, and was surprised to see her companions and the Aziza warriors heed her command. Even the Gazella paused. Weapons at the ready, Asha and her army stood and waited.

The rider drew closer. Asha could not see a face, only shadow.

Several feet away now, the rider pulled back the reins of his horse, stopped, and dismounted.

He was clad in black armor, and upon his face was a

mask of feathers. A deadly beak pointed from where his nose should be.

It was the Shrike.

What remained of his army immediately fell in behind him, fearless again now that their leader had arrived.

He stopped in front of Asha. "So you have come," he said.

Asha held Frost tightly but didn't answer. Rima, Obo, Pulligan, and the others watched closely. Sabra and Kalasha bounced on their toes, ready to strike at Asha's command.

The Shrike's eyes glinted from within the tangle of feathers. Asha felt them find hers. "A child?" he scoffed. "Born to throw me down? So much for prophecy."

His foul creatures laughed behind him.

He is my brother, Asha thought.

But before she had time to form a response, the Shrike leapt at her, sword upraised. Asha pivoted to her left, avoiding the blow. Obo, Sabra, and Kalasha rushed forward.

"No!" Pulligan called out to them. "This is Asha's moment. Only she can do this."

The warriors stepped back quickly, but their faces showed their eagerness to fight.

Asha and the Shrike began to circle one another slowly. Obo curled his whip in his hand, almost snarling.

Asha continued her dance around the Shrike, her brother. Maybe she could reason with him. She didn't want to kill him. She wasn't even sure she could.

He charged at her with his sword again, but, just as before, she raised her spear and blocked the blow, sending him reeling back. Frost seemed to vibrate in her hands, and sparks flew from it, even though it was made from wood.

Asha thrust forward, and the Shrike moved back. "I don't want to fight!" she shouted.

The Shrike smiled beneath his mask. Asha could see the upturn to the corners of his lips. "Are you afraid, child?" he asked, then dropped and spun with his legs out, sweeping Asha's feet out from under her.

Rima leapt forward, but Pulligan pulled her back. "This is madness!" she cried. "I swore to protect her!"

"It is her destiny!" Pulligan said firmly. "It has been foretold."

Rima shook her head in frustration.

Sprix bared his teeth and growled, and began stalking around Asha and the Shrike, watching every movement.

Asha leapt to her feet. The Shrike had an opening to

kill her, but he didn't. Why? Was he toying with her? Asha felt her breath coming in short bursts. Cold sweat trickled down her back. She knew she would be helpless without Frost. Whatever power it possessed had fused with her, giving her strength and confidence.

The Shrike moved slowly, back on his feet, looking for an opening, a weakness. He was small, Asha saw, smaller than she'd imagined he would be. They were almost the same height. "I could end you now if I wished," he threatened her, continuing his stealthy dance around her.

"Try it," Sabra countered, "and you'll be dead in an instant." She curled her rope around her wrist.

And then, the Shrike did something that no one expected.

He stepped back a pace.

He opened his mouth.

And he screamed.

TWENTY-THREE

THE FIERY HAND

S HRIKES.

Thousands of shrieking birds descended from the tower in answer to their master's call. They came swooping down like a great black cloud and dove at the Aziza, biting, cawing, and pecking.

A line of Tokoloshe rushed to form a defensive barrier in front of the Shrike as he continued his deadly call.

Obo, Rima, and Sprix dove back into the battle.

And the Shrike kept screaming.

The more he screamed, the more of his terrible flock answered. Soon, the plain was black as night, the sky blotted out by their wings.

Now as the terrible birds dove to earth, several of them turned into men, robed in black, just like the ones Asha had seen when her camp was attacked. But this time, she had a weapon, and vengeance was her ally.

Something inside her awakened at that moment—something much older than her few years. Deep within her was a seed of power only just now beginning to bloom. She felt it first in her ears, a ringing that grew in volume, louder and louder and louder. She recalled Pulligan's words when she told him she had no power: *Within you lies the power of a thousand suns.*

Asha batted the shrikes away as they dove and pecked at her head. She had to do something. And quickly. The shadowy figures in black were getting the best of the small Aziza warriors and her friends. They swarmed the Gazella, bringing down two, then three.

She gripped Frost with both hands and thought back to her Telling Day, when Suna touched her forehead and blessed her in the name of the Five.

"Royal Lioness," Asha whispered, raising the spear above her head. "Give me strength!"

She slammed Frost down into the earth.

A wave of light erupted from the ground, sending

out a cascade of fire and blue flame. Columns of smoke rose into the air, and the shrikes faltered, retreating back to the tower.

Asha stood frozen. The gods had heard her call. Or maybe she had the power inside her all along, waiting to be unleashed. All she needed to do was call upon it.

She focused her attention on the Shrike. He was bent over, coughing, his screeching silenced. The ground before his feet was split open from Asha's blow. Many of his foul warriors had fallen into it, shadow men and Tokoloshe. Now the others seemed to pause their attack, fearful.

Asha took the moment of surprise and ran forward with all the speed she could muster, spear held at her waist, and knocked the Shrike's feet out from under him. "Enough!" she shouted, standing over him, Frost's gleaming tip just inches from his throat. "Enough!"

All went silent. The Tokoloshe fell quiet. The cries of shrikes in the distance faded. The Aziza picked themselves up, as did the remaining enemy forces.

The Shrike lay on the ground, breathing hard.

Asha raised the spear.

She had to do it. For her mother. For her father. And for Suna.

I am sorry, she told herself.

She brought the spear down.

And thrust it into the earth again.

This time, no wave of light erupted. No one moved. A stillness settled over the carnage.

Asha blew out a breath, then bent down and pulled the mask of feathers from the Shrike's face.

She gasped.

What she saw before her was not a monster out of nightmares. It was a boy. A beautiful boy with jet-black curls and fine, sharp features. He looked a little like her, she realized. But how was this possible? He should be older, a grown man by now.

She stared into his eyes. "I will not kill you . . . brother."

The Shrike looked at her, his gaze still fierce. "I have no family."

But as Asha was about to answer, the air suddenly rippled around them. She tensed. Pulligan and his warriors stood alert, eyes darting to and fro.

Asha turned left, then right, trying to figure out what was happening. She could feel the air stirring the fine hair at the nape of her neck. Then something materialized out of the murkiness. Even the Tokoloshe looked frightened and huddled together, observing this new threat.

"What devilry is this?" Obo asked.

It was a man, Asha saw, or at least it looked like a man, dressed in robes of black and with a circlet of thorned vines around his head. Fissures of red, like fire, rippled across his skin. "Adisa," the stranger whispered.

The Shrike raised his head, his eyes red and unfocused. "Bazaal. Come at last."

Bazaal. Asha remembered the name. Pulligan had spoken of him when telling the story of the Shrike.

It was then that Adisa met in the woods a powerful sorcerer called Bazaal. He instilled in him a hatred of the Aziza people so fierce that Adisa's blood boiled. He told him that it was the Aziza who made him this way. The side of him he thought weak and ugly was all their doing.

"So you remember me," Bazaal said.

Asha thought she saw flames in his mouth, but she wasn't sure.

The Shrike didn't answer.

"I have come to finally collect that which was promised."

"What?" the Shrike said, exhausted. "What did I promise?"

Bazaal raised his chin, imperious. "Why, your soul, of course."

The Shrike lowered his head, and it was then that Asha saw what he truly was: her brother, enchanted, trapped in the body of a thirteen-year-old boy. For when he promised his soul to Bazaal, he became a thrall, a mere shadow of his former self, never to grow old, never to lead a long and happy life.

"You will not touch him," Asha said.

Bazaal turned to her. "The sister," he said. "Come to fulfill the prophecy." Asha gripped Frost and felt its energy coursing through her body.

"Extracting a soul is a . . . lengthy process," Bazaal said. "Would you like to see?"

Asha planted her feet wide apart and gripped Frost even tighter. "I do not fear you," she said, although she felt her arms trembling. Whether it was the power of Frost or her own nerves she did not know.

Bazaal didn't reply, only turned and faced Pulligan and the Aziza. "Ah, the small ones. The fool child thought you were to blame for his perceived . . . *flaws*. I only told him what he wanted to hear. His soul was already corrupted before he promised it to me. Would you like to see, too? Watch."

Pulligan held up a hand, holding back his warriors, who were poised with their spears, ready to attack.

I'm the one who has to stop him, it dawned on Asha. *It's the prophecy. It has to be me.*

The demon called Bazaal lifted his hands. Flame erupted from his palms.

"No!" the Shrike cried out, grasping his sword and awkwardly rising to his feet. Asha looked at her brother. For a moment, they were just that, brother and sister, and whatever bond they'd missed out on in life came to them right then, if only for an instant.

Now, Asha thought.

She swung Frost the same time her brother lifted his sword, bringing it down upon Bazaal.

Bazaal's face showed more shock than pain, as if he were surprised that someone so small could deign to strike him. The demon cried out and fell, but not before reaching out to touch the Shrike with a fiery hand.

Flames spread across the Shrike's frame. Asha rushed to his side. "Adisa!" she cried out. *That's his name. Not Shrike. Adisa.*

"Adisa!" she called again, but the boy who was her brother did not respond. Asha saw red streaks running through his skin, a web of darkness consuming him.

Asha turned to Bazaal, enraged. "No!" she cried as she twirled Frost above her head. The words came back to her then—words she had used twice before. "Back to the darkness!" she shouted and swung Frost with all her might.

Bazaal threw his hands up, but it was too late.

Asha delivered a killing blow, and the demon burst into flame. Tendrils of smoke spiraled into the air.

Pulligan and the Aziza looked on in surprised fascination, while Obo, Rima, and Sprix remained motionless, as if they were in shock. Asha rushed back and knelt at her brother's side. She remembered doing the same thing when Suna fell, looking into her green-flecked eyes. "Brother!" she said, cradling his head. "Adisa!"

Adisa smiled for a brief moment and Asha smoothed the curls away from his forehead. "I am sorry, sister," he said. "Forgive me. Please."

Asha felt her eyes welling up for a brother she didn't know. "I forgive you," she said. "Adisa."

Asha called for water but he waved her away, as if he knew his fate. Black and red lines traveled up from his neck to his face, like a deadly spiderweb. "Mother and Father. They are inside the tower. Tell them . . . tell them . . ."

And then he closed his eyes.

Asha stayed with him for what seemed like several

minutes but was surely only seconds. He seemed peaceful now. At last.

Light footfalls sounded behind her. "It is done, Empress," Pulligan said.

"Not yet," Asha answered. "My mother and father are in there. I have to find them."

TWENTY-FOUR

SHE WHO BRINGS LIGHT

WITH NO MASTER TO COMMAND them, what remained of the Tokoloshe scattered, some running away to who knew where, others watching Asha from a distance, as if she were their new leader. The mysterious black-robed creatures were gone, as well as the dragonflies and their riders. It was as if their power had been fueled by Bazaal, and with his death, they ceased to exist in this world, or went back into the shadows from where they came. Bazaal's end had lifted a spell that had Adisa and his minions in his grip.

Asha heard steps behind her, but they were not made

by a human. She turned around to find Toru surveying the battlefield and the ones he had lost. Asha felt terrible that some of the magnificent creatures would no longer roam the forest.

"Thank you, Great Forest Father," she said, bowing her head.

Toru's eyes still held the same mysterious gleam as they had before, but this time, Asha thought she saw sadness in them, too.

"Empress," he said. The deep rumble of his voice put Asha at ease for a moment. She wanted to reach out and touch him, to comfort him somehow, but she didn't know if it was the right thing to do.

She looked beyond Toru at the dead and wounded. "I am sorry for your losses," she said. "They were all brave to come to our aid."

"It is the last battle," Toru said. "My kind will no longer roam Alkebulan, for our true home is beyond this world."

Asha didn't really understand, but she nodded.

"We will not meet again, child," Toru told her. "Rule the kingdom with peace. Long may you reign."

And then he bounded off, calling his captains to his side.

Asha watched as the dust from the plain of battle rose under their feet.

She and her companions met no resistance as she led her Aziza warriors to the tower. Obo and Rima were by her side, bruised but not yet defeated. Sprix, now back in his human form and wearing Aziza clothing gathered from the supplies they carried, walked with a limp. Sabra and Kalasha remained close, still wary of any threat that would harm their empress.

Obo was still breathing hard. Blood spattered his shirt. Asha looked for signs of injury, but none were to be found. He opened and closed his mouth several times, as if searching for the right words. "I am sorry, Asha," he finally said.

"As am I," she answered.

And it was true.

She was sorry that her only brother was dead, and that he had been under the thrall of a demon.

"In the end . . ." Obo began, then paused thoughtfully. "He came around in the end. He asked for forgiveness."

"He was the Shrike," Asha replied.

"Yes, he was."

"But he was still my brother."

Asha thought for a moment about what it would have

been like if her brother had never left home. He would have welcomed her as his little sister, and none of this would have happened. In her mind's eye she saw her mother and father with her and Adisa, playing games, growing up together. She sighed at what had been lost. All because he had been teased and bullied. A child's hurt and anger that turned into a nightmare for thousands.

The sky was clear now that the battle was over. The tower was just ahead of them, and with each step, Asha's heart beat faster. *I will see my parents. Adisa said they are alive.*

Pulligan had sent half of his force to aid the wounded, while he and the other half accompanied Asha. He joined Asha and her friends as she led them forward. Blood stained his hands and his face showed signs of weariness. "We are victorious, Empress. A hard battle, but we are victorious."

Asha only nodded. She didn't know what to say. Battle meant death. It wasn't like in the stories. It was a terrible thing to see and experience. Still, her brother had found peace in the end. And for that she could find some happiness.

The dull iron doors of the tower were only steps

away. They approached warily, although whatever sorcery had protected it was now gone. Up close, Asha saw that the tower seemed to be made of some type of black rock, pockmarked with dents and rivets. She reached out and touched the surface, which was cold.

She turned around to face her companions and Pulligan. "Follow me," she said. She studied the surviving Aziza warriors. *Her* warriors, battered and bloodstained. "The rest of you keep watch here. If we do not return soon, do not follow. We will face our own fate."

Pulligan looked at her then, and it was with a new expression, one that Asha could only call respect.

Inside, she led them along a stone passageway emblazoned with the image of the mask Adisa had worn upon his face, feathers and a sharp-beaked nose.

"They're probably in a dungeon," Rima said. "I feel cool air. This way."

They found a staircase of winding stone steps that seemed to go on forever and followed it down. Torches affixed to the walls provided enough light to see that the stones were wet and slick with a green moss. Asha almost lost her footing several times. The farther they descended, the damper the air became.

Finally, Asha stepped down onto the cold, damp

floor. They were in a long room that had closed doors with iron bands across them at either end.

"Could they be in there?" Sprix asked. Asha saw that his limp was worse. *Should have left him with the others,* she thought. *For his own safety.* She could still see his fox-self in her mind's eye. It was extraordinary.

She stared at the doors, hoping Sprix was wrong. She couldn't imagine spending a life locked away in such a manner—to not feel the fresh air on your face; to only have four walls as your whole existence.

"One way to find out," Obo declared. He lifted his pine staff and banged it against one of them. The sound echoed and faded.

Asha listened for any sign of life. None came.

But then . . .

A scuttling from behind the door.

"There's someone in there!" Rima whispered.

Asha's heart raced in her chest. "Stand back."

She lifted Frost, which flared with its cold, fierce light. With one deafening strike, she thrust the spear forward, as if attacking an opponent. A blue flash erupted from it, and the iron bands across the door split asunder.

Obo and Pulligan pulled away the splintered metal and wood. Asha realized her hands were shaking with anticipation. Or maybe it was the reverberation from Frost's blow.

She stepped forward into the room slowly to get a look.

Two skeletons clung to each other in a final embrace.

"That can't be them," Asha cried. "It can't be! He said they were alive. Adisa told me they were inside!"

A rat scurried from the darkness and raced through the door.

"Come," Obo said. "We have to keep looking."

They tried the door at the other end, but it opened to a room that was empty except for a table and chair. A broken water pitcher lay on the floor. Asha wondered what kind of horror had taken place there.

"Look," Pulligan said, stepping farther into the room. "There is another hall here."

They all huddled around Pulligan. Asha looked past him down a long, dark tunnel. Blackness loomed ahead.

Asha gripped her staff. She closed her eyes. "Please work," she said softly, and then, "Light."

She opened her eyes to see Frost's point glowing, and sighed a breath of relief. "Come," she said, stepping into the tunnel. "I have to find them."

The passageway was narrow and they all had to walk

single file, with Asha at the front. Their steps echoed.

"Where could they be?" Asha asked.

Then, as if in answer, she heard a soft voice. It was singing. Someone was singing.

A memory tickled her brain.

. . . one morning, a young Aziza woman named Amira was gathering fruit from the marula tree. She loved to sing, and on this day, her voice carried throughout the forest until it reached the ears of a human man named Saka.

Asha paused. *Could it be? Mother?*

"This way!" she said, quickening her pace.

The voice lifted on the air and seemed to come from everywhere at once: above and below, left and right. She felt as if it were calling out to her. Beckoning.

The tunnel led to another flight of stone steps and Asha rushed down them, not even waiting for her companions.

The song became more vibrant; high, then low. Around a corner, and Asha paused. There, in a room that contained only a small bed and two chairs, a man and woman sat. Asha knew it was her parents. They had to be.

The woman looked up from her singing. Her hair was unkempt and her face thin. Asha immediately saw that she was Aziza. Not only because of her size, but her large eyes had the same slow-blinking rhythm as Pulligan's. Asha saw herself and her brother in that face.

Next to her was a man with hair in unkempt braids. He was taller than the woman, but not by much. He had kind eyes, Asha saw, even after all this time. Shock was etched on both of their faces.

"Asha?" the woman said, rising up.

Asha felt her mouth go dry.

The man, surely her father, rose from his chair. He gazed at her intently. "Asha," he said, his voice breaking. "You have come."

"She is Empress," Pulligan said, stepping into the small room. "She Who Brings Light."

TWENTY-FIVE

EMPRESS

B EFORE ASHA HAD TIME to figure out how it happened, she was embracing her mother and father. *I don't want to let go*, she thought. *Ever.*

"Adisa," her father said at last, breaking their embrace. "My son. Is he . . . ?"

"Yes," Asha answered sadly. "By the hand of a demon."

Amira hung her head and wept for her son—the boy who had been led astray. Saka held her close and wept also. Asha hurt to see them cry. She couldn't imagine what they had gone through—to be held prisoner by their own child.

"He asked for forgiveness," she finally managed to say. "He was corrupted by an evil that fed on his anger and self-doubt."

Amira, with tears in her eyes, looked to Asha. "How are you here?"

"We must go now, Empress," Pulligan said suddenly, looking around warily. "There are still Tokoloshe about. We must leave this place."

Asha's mother turned to Pulligan, as if seeing him for the first time. "Empress," she whispered. Her eyes shifted to Sabra and Kalasha. Recognition suddenly seemed to dawn on her face. "My people," she said softly. "My people."

"Yes," Pulligan told her. "We have not forgotten you, Amira."

Asha gripped Frost tighter and led her parents from the dark underbelly of Shrike's nest, and up into daylight.

As they left the barren plain and began their journey back to the Aziza's Underground Kingdom, Asha caught her parents up on everything. First, she told them of Suna and her death.

"She was a brave and intelligent woman," her father

said in a pained voice.

Sadness filled Amira's eyes. "I remember Suna well. She always had a kind word whenever she saw us. She and some of the others from her troupe came to our aid when we were . . . attacked."

"She did everything she could to keep me safe," Asha said. "Until the end."

"She raised you well," her mother added. "I wish I could have . . . I could only get you to safety, Asha, when Adisa sent those . . ." Tears glistened on her cheeks.

Asha reached out and grasped her hand. "I know," she said calmly. "You did the right thing, Mother."

Amira smiled through her tears and squeezed back.

Asha continued her tale. She told them about her Telling Day and her mark; her escape with Obo and meeting Rima and Sprix. Lastly, she spoke of the Gazella and the Golden Path, and how she eventually found Pulligan. The whole while, Amira and Saka listened intently. Shock, pride, and relief played across their faces.

They collected Adisa's body and buried him far from the Burned Lands, under a marula tree by a swift-running stream. "He liked the water," Saka said. "When he was little."

"Here he will rest," Rima added.

Asha remembered the words she'd said over the lifeless body of Suna. It seemed so long ago. "Royal Lioness," she began quietly, repeating them now. "Goddess of Life and Death. Please take our brother and son into your great dominion. Watch over him and keep him safe on his journey." She swallowed back tears. "By the Five."

"By the Five," echoed the others.

As they continued their journey home, Asha had plenty of questions for her mother and father. There was so much she didn't know.

"Where we found you," she began. "What was that place? You were not in a prison. Why?"

Saka let out a sigh. "Adisa kept us there for a very long time. Every few days he would let us out into the open air, but we could never escape. His guards were always watching."

"It was as if he didn't want us to suffer," Amira added, "but he didn't want to let us go, either."

Asha shook her head at the madness of it all.

After many days of travel, they found their way back to the Underground Kingdom at last. There, Pulligan gathered all of the Aziza in the great cavern around the Mother Tree.

"There is no need to hide any longer," Pulligan said to them.

And it was true.

The Shrike was defeated.

The Aziza tribes left their homes underground and lived among the stars and sky once again. Tree, root, and rock remained their refuge, but not their prison.

The Baobab Circle Tribe made a forest home near a stream and a grove of moringa trees. It was bountiful there, with food, shelter, and water. They lived off the harvest of the land, as they used to, before the reign of the Shrike.

Asha spoke with her parents as often as she could, during the day and sometimes long into the night. Their ordeal had taken a toll on them. It took a while for their strength to return, but with the help of the Aziza, who tended to them with great care, they soon felt at ease in the world again.

One evening, Asha awoke to find Sabra and Kalasha by her bedside. She looked at both of them with curiosity. "Um, can I help you with something?" she asked.

The two young women dipped their heads and placed a hand on their hearts. "Forgive me, Empress, but you must come," Kalasha said.

"I must, must I?" Asha said jokingly, rising out of bed and throwing on something more presentable than her sleeping clothes. "Well, then. I guess I'd better hurry."

Sabra and Kalasha led Asha away.

"Where are you taking me?" she asked, not really irritated, but curious.

The two young women didn't reply, but led her along a path to the cavern where she'd first seen all the Aziza tribes gathered together. Asha stopped and gasped. The whole of the Rowan Circle Tribe, as well as the Chestnut Clan, the Moringa Spears, the Ivy Grove, and the Baobab Circle, stood quietly, waiting for her arrival. Pulligan was there, as were Obo and Rima. Asha saw that Sprix no longer walked with a limp. Her mother and father, now much healthier and with faces full of joy, gazed at their daughter lovingly.

"What . . . what is going on?" Asha asked.

Pulligan came forth. He wore a circlet of leaves around his head. "An empress cannot truly reign without a crown."

At those words, as if on cue, Amira and Saka walked toward her, followed by Obo, Rima, and Sprix.

"Today," Pulligan said, "we crown an empress of the Aziza. The first of her kind. Asha, She Who Brings Light."

He bowed his head.

Asha was taken aback. She'd barely had time to rub the sleep from her eyes. She nudged Sabra. "Why didn't you warn me?"

Sabra only smiled and covered her mouth with her hand. Kalasha couldn't hide her joy, and laughed aloud.

Asha felt emotion flood her body as her parents drew closer. Her father held something in his hands, which he gave to Asha's mother.

"Daughter," Amira said. "With this, I crown you Empress of the Aziza."

Amira raised the crown. It was carved from a soft white wood, and intricate marks were etched upon its surface. She placed it upon Asha's head.

Asha raised her chin and smiled.

"Behold!" Pulligan announced. "Asha, Empress of the Aziza!"

Asha felt every eye on her as the crowd cheered.

Obo grinned and hoisted his pine staff in the air.

Pulligan approached and offered his hand. "A coronation is not complete without a celebration."

That's when Asha saw that the path before her was strewn with black flowers from the Mother Tree. A tent of white cloth had been set up and several Aziza gathered around it. Platters of food and drink were waiting. The sound of pipes and drums floated through the trees, as it had long, long ago.

"After you, Empress," Pulligan said.

As Asha walked along the path in her bare feet, she was joined by her companions, Obo, Rima, and Sprix.

And on that day, a new empress ruled in Alkebulan.

Later, as they all sat before a fire, Asha's mother took a length of Asha's hair in her hands. "I've always wanted to comb my daughter's hair. May I?"

Asha smiled.

"Yes," she said, happily. "Yes, you may, Mother."